AT OCEAN'S DOOR

JAKKI JELENE

ISBN: 978-1-954771-00-0

This book is a work of fiction. Names, characters, places, and incidents are the product of the author's imagination or are used fictitiously. Any resemblance to actual events, locales, or persons, living or dead, is coincidental.

Cover Design: Jakki Jelene
Cover Image: Atıf Zafrak

Published in the United States of America

www.jakkijelene.com

"The heart of man is very much like the sea, it has its storms, it has its tides and in its depths it has its pearls too."

– *Vincent van Gogh*

CHAPTER ONE

N oah Sullivan's earliest memory was of the sea. Its sights and sounds had always been before him, but its salty taste had never touched his tongue. He spent the entirety of his youth at Birchwood Cottage which was a mere fifty yards off the rocky Maine coast in the small town of Newland. His father, Martin, had the cottage built shortly after he married Noah's mother, Grace, and they remained there even after her untimely death in which she succumbed to a terrible bout of pneumonia the winter following Noah's birth.

The home was a large stone cottage lined with rows of

pretty, arched lattice windows, surrounded by trees, and looked like something out of a storybook. The front, which faced away from the ocean, had a circle drive that met up with an arched double mahogany front door, which opened to a small foyer that expanded into a warm and inviting hall and dining room. Deeper within the home were four spacious bedrooms and two enormous sitting-rooms on either end of the house. In the back were several arched windows that faced the ocean, and in the center, two French doors opened to a large terrace with a stunning view of the sea where Noah often spent his time in the summer months.

Noah's father was a fisherman by trade, and because the home held too many painful memories of his late wife, he was eager to head back out to sea in hopes of taking his mind off the pain of losing the only woman he had ever loved. In doing so, Noah was left to be tended to by his Aunt Priscilla, Prissy as most people called her, for she was Martin's younger sister and most faithful companion now that Grace was gone. Martin made Prissy promise to look after his son while he was away to ensure his safety as he claimed he could not bear the thought of anything happening to him too. As she was unmarried and completely devoted to her brother, it was an oath Prissy took deadly serious and so Noah's entire childhood was intensely sheltered.

Most days Noah spent lazing away in his large bedroom and joint sitting-room, furnished suitably for an indefinite stay. It was stocked with all the creature comforts necessary to keep him distracted from the lure of the outside world and over the years Noah remained feeble in both body and mind. Unable to cope with the regularity of his demands and childish outbursts, Aunt Prissy often locked herself away in her own wing of the house to calm her fragile nerves.

They were routinely aroused by other concerns as well. Noah was easily chilled and prone to suffer severely from the most common of colds and Aunt Prissy often panicked at any sign of sickness. Therefore, she continued to perpetuate the notion that home was the only place that offered safety and security. This suited young Noah just fine as he kept himself busy enough with the many amusements she provided as a result.

Though not very accomplished in much of his schoolwork, for Noah severely lacked discipline, he naturally took to painting and became increasingly proficient at it. Noah's tutor, the highly regarded Miss Weathervane, was quite impressed with his use of color and dimension, despite him still being what she called, a "dauber." She was by far the toughest of all his tutors so that he was always immensely pleased when he would earn her praise for his work. This constant challenge was the only thing that motivated him toward improvement and despite the tendency to hold back her approval, soon even Miss Weathervane could not hide her astonishment regarding his rapidly growing skills.

As a result, painting was Noah's greatest source of joy and he came to love nothing better than to sit at his easel and be overtaken by the hypnotic roar of the waves in the distance while he labored away on his latest piece. This not only served him well for the creative outlet painting provided to his dull life, but also that it turned his eyes and ears to the beauty of the outside world, something he had never taken much notice of. It was only when he was painting that Noah would go to the terrace and spend time in the fresh sea air among the glorious backdrop of Maine.

The backyard of the cottage was modest in size, yet spacious enough to roam among the lush gardens Aunt Prissy tended to while watching the birds and butterflies that would frequently stop by for a visit. This year the garden was popping with pink roses, yellow daffodils, blue forget-me-nots, red daylilies, and a variety of pansies—all contained within the green hedges lining the property that divided the land from the seagrass at the edge of the sandy shore. Some almost believed Aunt Prissy to possess a special magic that brought the garden to life as she would regularly place first in the county fair for horticulture and would share her secrets with no one.

Though there were several homes stretched out on either side of the property, the cottage was largely isolated from the townspeople. Noah rarely saw much activity as the local beach, marina and market were where most people congregated. Noah had only been to town a few times in his young life before Aunt Prissy decided to halt his trips altogether following a terrible cough he developed, which she blamed on their last trip to the market. So, Noah became content with the rugged, lonely piece of coastal paradise where he resided. That was until the day *she* appeared.

It was a sight he'd never forget. Noah was all of sixteen now and figured she must be about his age, perhaps a year younger. She was an enchanting creature, bounding with endless joy that seemed to cause a golden light to emanate from her being. Her soft brown curls fell just past her fair shoulders which were covered only by the ruffled straps of her lavender sundress. She carried a small white basket and glided along the shore, stopping every so often to pick something up to place inside it. He wondered what she was gathering and wished to ask but was frozen with fear and fascination.

Noah had seen few girls his age, aside from the Reverend Thomas's daughters, Ruth and Leah, who were pale and cheerless with upturned noses. Leah was a few years younger, but Ruth, the one closest to his age, would often watch him closely with a curious look on her face. He would stare back waiting for her to speak, but she never did, and he marveled at what a strange girl she appeared to be.

He had read about romance in books but for the life of him could not understand the appeal of girls when Ruth and Leah came to visit. He could not even consider them friends, as they were simply doing the "Lord's work", as Mrs. Thomas called it, by checking in on local folk that had fallen to some misfortune. Mrs. Thomas would sometimes gaze upon Noah with pitying eyes, urge Aunt Prissy to come to church service on Sunday, then leave behind a less than appetizing fruit basket.

Aunt Prissy was always polite during these occasional visits, but as soon as the Reverend, his wife, and two daughters left the house she would turn with an exasperated sigh and murmur something to herself about the problem with "sanctimonious self-righteous saints" and how they were only interested in finding new things to gossip about. Noah thought to himself that the joke must be on them since nothing new ever happened at Birchwood Cottage worth talking about.

But this girl was quite different than any he had ever

encountered. Even from his vantage point, he was mesmerized by the bright and sunny smile that adorned her round, flushed face. She was enjoying her simple task more than he'd ever seen anyone enjoy anything at all. And so, he watched as she continued gathering until a voice called out to her from down the beach, a name he couldn't quite distinguish, that caused her to run back in the direction she came.

Noah wistfully contemplated the possibility that he might never see this fascinating creature again and wondered if she had been nothing more than an apparition. But two days later as he sat on the terrace painting a stormy sky on a coastal horizon, he saw her dancing his way once again, her peals of laughter carrying on the wind, and just as before, he was captivated by the beauty of her blithe spirit.

She didn't carry a basket with her this time, but instead wore a bright yellow bathing suit, and on her head was a white sunhat with a wide brim. Her parents followed behind, walking slowly and deep in conversation. She ran to a spot close to where the waves crested, laid out what looked to be an old quilt, then removed her sunhat, and seconds later she went bounding toward the waves and dove in without hesitation. If the water was cold, you wouldn't know it by the way she took to it so quickly. She was truly alive and clearly in her element as she jumped playfully into the waves, shrieking with delight as each crashed over her. Her soft curls were now a thick, mass of wet ringlets which was no less beautiful than they were a moment before.

Her parents continued past her and walked on toward the other end of the shore, seemingly unconcerned with her being alone in the massive, powerful ocean. Noah couldn't imagine such freedom as he had never so much as dipped his toe in the surf; only watched safely from his window or terrace. He now wished he could join the girl in what looked like magnificent fun!

Noah thought perhaps he might one day ask Aunt Prissy if he might take a swim in the sea but knew the answer at once. Still, it did not stop him from daydreaming about it. How delightful it would be if he could arrange to meet this girl, he mused. For now, he simply observed her every move, not yet finding the courage to make himself known. He tried to memorize her features even from afar, for surely, he would think of nothing else the rest of the day and night.

CHAPTER TWO

A few days passed and Noah was disappointed to find no sign of the mysterious young girl. Dark clouds were looming over the sea which promised rain, so Aunt Prissy urged Noah to stay indoors and forgo painting on the terrace that afternoon. Instead, he set up his easel in his sitting-room near the window, mixing black and white paints in an attempt to create the perfect stormy hue for the piece he had already begun.

While still in the process of mixing the paints, he casually looked up at the sky in the distance when he saw the movement of a figure below in his peripheral—it was *her*! The girl was barefoot with a flowing pink dress, a white shawl wrapped around her ever-bronzing shoulders. She was alone and watching the approaching clouds, wind whipping wildly through her chestnut locks. Her hands stretched out in opposite directions, each holding a corner of the shawl as she welcomed the breeze with open arms. She began jumping and twirling as sand flew about her when she suddenly turned to look at Birchwood Cottage as if noticing it for the first time.

The windows reflected the light of day so she did not notice the boy staring back at her, but as Noah focused on the girl observing his home, he unconsciously stepped closer to the window so that she could now make out his figure slightly. Enough to know it was a boy, though his face was still quite indiscernible.

Taking notice that she was being watched, the girl raised her right arm and waved exuberantly to Noah. It startled him at first, realizing she had spotted him, so he stepped back briefly. It wasn't exactly how he pictured revealing himself to her, but he quickly regained his senses and stepped forward to the window again, waving in return. Realizing the moment might soon turn awkward, and for fear the girl would leave again, Noah acted swiftly and slid the window up so he could speak. Even so, he surprised himself to hear his voice calling out a friendly, "hello." The bubbly girl eagerly greeted him with a "hello" in return.

"From the looks of those clouds, it seems there will be a good deal of rain coming any minute. It would be quite silly of you to stay on the beach much longer." Noah cringed at his own words, realizing he not only insulted this potential friend but might chase her away for good. But it honestly did seem a foolish thing to remain on the beach during a storm and for that reason, he expected the interaction wouldn't last long at any rate.

The girl shouted back against the ever-increasing wind, but he could make out her words just the same, "Yes, I know I am quite silly, but I haven't far to go! My family just moved into the little blue cottage next door. My name is Lily Stephens, what's your name?"

Due to the trees lining the property, Noah couldn't recall even knowing what the house next door looked like, least of all what color it was. Still, it was pleasing news to know they had a new friendly neighbor who would stick around a while. "My name is Noah Sullivan," he called back, "and I live here with my aunt!"

"Nice to meet you, Noah," she called out, "Perhaps I'll get a chance to meet your aunt as well sometime." She flashed a cheeky smile. A light sprinkling of rain began at that moment and Lily knew she'd have to run home before the deluge, but not before further pressing the issue, "Would it be okay to stop by and meet properly sometime?"

Noah thought for a moment then said, "Yes, I suppose that would be alright. How about tomorrow at noon, before my painting lessons?"

Lily clapped her hands together enthusiastically then responded, "Yes, I will see you tomorrow then, Noah Sullivan. Goodbye!" The wind suddenly gained even greater strength, so she waved and ran off just before heavy rain began pouring over the entire region.

CHAPTER THREE

I t was a quarter to noon the following day and the sun had reemerged from the overcast sky of the previous day. Noah paced anxiously in his sitting-room awaiting news of his guest's arrival. When Noah informed Aunt Prissy of the sudden visitor he was expecting she told him that she would have to think it over before giving her final approval. Noah had never received a visitor of his own before, aside from the Reverend and his daughters, so Aunt Prissy never considered such a prospect. Even though the risk of spreading sickness was ever-present, July was not a high-risk month for cold and flu. Since Noah had been quite hearty recently, she ultimately concluded that there was no legitimate reason to keep him from having a new friend over and she gave her consent to the meeting with the promise that the girl would not stay more than an hour.

When the clock struck noon, Noah began feeling a bit queasy. He was nervous about how he would present himself as he wanted to make a good impression. For the occasion, he chose to wear a neatly pressed, black button-up shirt, and beige trousers. His usually shaggy blonde hair was combed neatly to one side and when he looked in the mirror earlier that morning his cool blue eyes reflected confidently back at him. Now he wasn't so sure of himself. He took another quick look in the mirror to confirm he was presentable and felt reassured that he was.

He didn't have much to compare himself to but considered himself to have pleasing features, save for his protruding toothy grin which he was told he inherited from his mother. Most people regarded Grace as quite the beauty while she was alive so he hoped he would soon grow into it and be handsome enough despite it. The clock moved a couple more minutes past twelve and Noah's spirits began to sink with the realization that Lily might not show up at all, when there was a knock at the front door.

Noah heard the muffle of voices in the hall when the

door to his sitting-room opened and Aunt Prissy ushered Lily in, proclaiming her arrival. He took in her every feature as he walked over to greet her and found Lily standing before him smiling sweetly with a plate of cookies in her hands. "Hello Noah, it's so nice to meet you," she said handing him the plate, "I brought a batch of my favorite cherry chip cookies for you and your Aunt, I do hope you will like them. They were always a hit back home. Please feel free to try one."

It was an unexpected, though welcome, surprise. He smiled at her kindly, "Thank you, Lily, what a thoughtful gesture. I certainly shall!" Noah reached out to take the plate from her and lifted a perfect looking cookie from the top and took a bite. It was still warm, indicating it was freshly baked, and somewhat chewy. "Wow," he exclaimed, "this is delicious! It might just be the best cookie I've ever had. You must try one, Aunt Prissy."

He handed the plate to his aunt, who took it and grimaced, "Perhaps later dear, I'm feeling out of sorts and I'm afraid my constitution can't handle it after this morning's breakfast. It was so very rich. How about I put this in the kitchen for now?" Prissy then left the room hastily.

Lily seemed pleased with herself just the same, "I'm so glad you liked it, it's my very own recipe! I can't cook a bit, but my Nana taught me to bake when I was a little girl and I very much enjoy it."

Noah was glad that he appeared to have rectified any previous offense for calling her 'silly' and proceeded to eat the rest of the cookie with much delight. He now had a chance to assess Lily up close and personal. She was even lovelier than he imagined. He wasn't sure if she would be classified as a beauty like his mother, but there was something immensely pleasant in her countenance and her eyes sparkled with joy when she smiled at him.

He wasn't familiar with proper etiquette but knew he must speak now as another moment of silence would probably appear rude and ungracious. He motioned to her to have a seat on the sofa in the sitting-room and proceeded to sit in the armchair across from it. "So, what brings you to Newland and where did you live before?"

Lily was happy to answer his question. "We used to live in Virginia, but papa had grown weary of working as an accountant for a shipbuilder. He was very good at it but decided to take a break from the pressure he was under. His family was originally from Maine, so he grew up in this region and had such fond memories that he decided to purchase the little blue cottage to spend the summer here while he figures out what to do next. It was all very sudden, but here we are!"

Noah's heart sank at the prospect that their stay may

only be temporary, "How are you liking Maine so far?"

"Oh, I just love it!" Lily gushed, "Though I wasn't sure I would. You see, I grew up near the sea in Virginia, but it is nowhere near as beautiful as it is here—and right at my doorstep! I could spend every summer day walking along the shore and swimming in the ocean. Couldn't you?"

Noah turned crimson, "Well, I don't know. I've never actually been down to the shore."

"What?" Lily could not hide her shock, "Never? How could you not when it's so very close?"

Noah had never thought to be embarrassed about his circumstance until now, and despite feeling self-conscious, tried his best to explain, "Well, the truth is, I'm not well. My Aunt Prissy forbids me from going because my father is concerned for my health."

"So, then your papa lives here too?"

"Well, yes and no. He is away a lot because he is a fisherman...a dang fine one at that! He usually comes home for a bit at the end of the season but then he's back to work fixing up fishing boats, traps and even doing some ice fishing before the season starts again. I don't see a lot of him, to be honest, but he takes good care of Aunt Prissy and I." Lily was quiet for a moment as she wondered about his mother, but before she could ask Noah added, "You see, my mother died shortly after I was born so it's difficult for him to be here."

"I'm so sorry Noah," Lily said softly.

"Well, I was just a baby, so I never knew her, but everyone says she was quite magnificent."

"I'm sure she was," Lily replied kindly then decided to switch to a lighter topic. "Well, you certainly have a lovely home here. Much bigger than ours. And this room is incredible—what a view!" She stood up and walked over to the large window where she had seen Noah peering out at her just the day before.

"It's all mine. Aunt Prissy has her own sitting-room. We dine together every evening, but aside from tutoring, I spend my time in here by myself." For some reason, his situation sounded incredibly lonely when he said it out loud, especially as he recognized the sympathy reflected in Lily's eyes when she turned to face him.

"Do you have many visitors?" she inquired further.

"Not really, just my tutors…and you."

Lily was sad to hear this but brightened the moment with her natural ability to move the conversation forward, "Well, that's just fine! I hope that means you won't mind me coming by again soon. You are my first and only friend since I've moved to Newland and I sure would love it if we could spend more time getting to know each other better."

Lily's enthusiasm in expressing her desire to visit again touched Noah's heart. "That would be fantastic, Lily. Perhaps it might be fun to have a companion for a change, someone to talk about things with other than Aunt Prissy and Reverend Thomas and his two sulky daughters." He couldn't believe he said that out loud.

"Who are the two daughters?" Lily asked.

"Ruth and Leah. They stop by on occasion, but they only come to check on people in town and are not really what I would consider friends. I'm sure you'll meet them soon enough. You're new here and they make it their business to know everybody in Newland. They are very dull though, not at all like you."

Noah blushed at his own words, but Lily laughed out loud at his remark. "Well hopefully they aren't as bad as all that. I guess we'll see soon enough!"

Noah realized how ungracious he must have seemed and figured he would have to work on his decorum if he hoped to keep Lily as a friend. Right now, he wanted that more than anything.

Noah and Lily spent the rest of the afternoon together engrossed in conversation. They asked each other a lot of questions regarding their upbringing and interests, and along with their love of the sea they found they had a couple of other delightful things in common; their favorite childhood book was Peter Pan by J.M. Barrie and both had an immense appreciation for art and painting. Noah also learned that History and French were Lily's favorite subjects in school, though he had no use for any of it himself. Noah never found any reason to put the knowledge he learned from his studies to use so instead he spent most of his time daydreaming during his lessons. He would often imagine the fantastic worlds he read about in books and longed to paint them.

More than once, Noah became frustrated with how little he was able to contribute to the topics Lily brought up, but she didn't seem to mind. Lily was always good at finding common ground and would simply change the subject if it didn't appear to interest Noah. Though she was surprised by how ignorant he was of the world, deep down Lily suspected Noah was much brighter than he seemed, though she didn't want to say so in case it might hurt his feelings.

Not being used to visitors, it wasn't long before Noah became fatigued. He thought perhaps it would be best to rest a bit before his painting lesson in an hour, which he politely explained to Lily but asked if she might visit again tomorrow so that they could resume their conversation. Noah was certain she couldn't have had much fun with him but was surprised when she didn't say no. Instead, Lily explained that she wouldn't be able to come back the next day, as she was heading to the city with her parents on a shopping trip, but that she would gladly stop by the following day. Noah was more than pleased with that and thanked her once again for coming and for the delicious cookies.

She smiled and took his hand to shake it before heading out and he could still feel her warm fingers wrapped around his even hours later. These new sensations were confusing, but oh so wonderful. Was this the thing he read about in all those books? He thought back a bit more on their conversation and wondered what sort of impression he left on her. He wasn't eloquent or charming. In truth, he was quite unskilled when it came to social graces. He contemplated whether he had been polite enough or came off as an unsophisticated dolt. But then, there was something so natural about Lily's demeanor that put him at ease, even when uncomfortable moments arose. She never seemed to indicate being displeased or perturbed by his unpolished manner. True he was no gentleman, but he hoped that perhaps one day his father would teach him better how to impress young ladies. After all, the man had caused his mother to fall madly in love with him, so he must know a thing or two.

These thoughts were suddenly interrupted by Aunt Prissy who knocked on the door then opened it without waiting for a response. "So how was your visit?" she asked pointedly.

"It went very well, I believe. In fact, she promises to visit again in two days."

His aunt was silent and thinking. "Are you sure that's a good idea?" she finally stated with a hint of concern.

Noah was confused, "Why wouldn't it be?"

"Well, a boy in your condition should be careful not to get overly excited. A new friendship could become overwhelming for your health, should the expectations of it cause you too much stress."

Noah hadn't considered that friendship could bring about any unpleasantness in his life, only joy and excitement. After all, Lily seemed more than willing to accommodate his needs. "I don't believe it will be a problem Aunt Prissy. Lily was quite kind and seems to understand my circumstance. I think it may actually do me quite a bit of good to have a friend."

"Well, you know my nerves, I worry for you as if you were my own son. Your poor father wouldn't know what to do if you suddenly became overwrought with emotion and suffered for it. It's my duty to keep you well and happy for his sake. Martin loves you so, as do I."

Noah could feel the heat rise to his cheeks at the

mention of his father and wanted to cry out, *Oh yeah, if he loves me so much, why doesn't he ever want to spend any time with me?* But he resisted knowing his poor aunt would only begin sobbing and remind Noah of the pain his father endured when his mother died and that everything he does is for his sake to make sure he is taken care of. Noah wasn't convinced of this, though he hoped it was true. He needed his father now more than ever and it saddened him to know it would still be at least a couple of months before he would return home.

"Please don't worry Aunt Prissy," he pleaded, "I will be alright, and nothing would be more wonderful than having someone my own age to talk with for a change. It can be so lonely here at times."

For all his effort not to hurt his aunt, she began to sob just the same, "I'm so sorry Noah that the company of an old woman just isn't enough for you. Just the same, I've always thought we were good friends, you and me. Haven't I cared for you like a mother? Even in your sickness? Haven't I done well to ensure you always had whatever you asked for, that you wanted for nothing? And yet I see it has not been enough. Perhaps I spoil you, but I couldn't bear to see you unhappy. Can't you see that everything I do for you is out of love?"

Noah stood from his chair and walked over to his aunt, putting his arms around her as he did as a boy. "Yes

Aunt, you have done well, and I love you dearly, but now I would like to have a real friend of my very own, just like so many other boys my age. You have your lady friends in town who visit often. Would it be so terrible if I had a friend come to call on occasion?"

Aunt Prissy hugged Noah back, for she enjoyed being the recipient of his sympathy. While she was diligent in keeping him well, she was also weak to his desires when he was generous with his affections. She truly did see him as her own son and often secretly wished he would call her "mother" but didn't dare say so, for she suspected Martin would not approve.

"Noah," she finally answered, "You are not like so many boys your age, and Lily is a girl, which complicates the matter, but still, I suppose it wouldn't hurt to consider it."

Noah knew this meant he won out and would be granted permission for Lily to continue visiting—at least for the time being. He was relieved to put the battle of convincing his aunt behind him so he could instead focus on preparing for Lily's next visit.

He suddenly got a second wind and instead of resting, began prepping for his upcoming painting lesson and decided that he would like to share some of his artwork with Lily. Hopefully, that would impress her! He didn't have a lot to show for his sixteen years on earth, but his progressing art skills was one area he did feel a little proud of.

CHAPTER FOUR

The next two days passed slowly, and Noah could hardly wait to see Lily again. He had thought a great deal about their first meeting and how kind and considerate she was. Unaccustomed as he was to desserts, he ate the entire plate of cookies without Aunt Prissy's help. He tried to convince her to take one, but she always refused, blaming it on one reason or another—her stomach was out of sorts, she had just eaten a bit of sweets, or she was watching her waistline—but Noah knew Aunt Prissy to never turn down baked goods and so he suspected she still didn't quite approve of this new friendship.

"She sure is a lovely sort of girl. Don't you agree Aunt Prissy?" he asked her at dinner later the first night.

"She seemed fine enough I suppose," she retorted, "though a bit too forward for a young lady if you ask me. I do wonder what kind of girl invites herself over to a young man's house without first being introduced to his guardian. I must say, girls these days behave more brazen than boys."

Noah didn't care what Aunt Prissy said though, he was smitten with this darling creature who suddenly waltzed into his life. He considered himself quite fortunate that she had shown interest in meeting him. *My painting may not be enough, I need to come up with some interesting topic of conversation for our next meeting*, he thought to himself. So, he spent some time in his library reading up on the state of Virginia and thought he might impress Lily with some new knowledge of her home state.

As the time drew closer to Lily's arrival, Noah began to wonder if he hadn't built her up in his mind, but once her smiling face was before him, he realized he hadn't recalled just how captivating she actually was. She arrived wearing a white sundress with her hair pulled pack into a bouncy ponytail, tied neatly with a light blue bow. Her chipper demeanor informed him that she too was quite glad to be in his company once again.

Lily was in high spirits and with wide, expressive eyes she spent the next fifteen minutes recounting her shopping trip and telling him all about the city and the sights she had seen. Even though the city was only eighteen miles away, Noah had never been, but she had a way of making him eager to see it for himself. Aunt Prissy had told him things about her trips, but it never interested him quite as it did when Lily described it. How grand and exciting it all seemed now!

Noah's sudden desire to visit the city gave him pause for he knew his aunt would be markedly against the idea. He then considered that perhaps now he was becoming a man and that his father might relent and allow Noah to come along on one of his many trips where he would stock up on supplies for the fishing season. Perhaps he would even be glad of Noah's interest in accompanying him. Surprisingly, it wasn't until that very moment that Noah had even contemplated the likelihood that his dad might one day wish to teach him his trade, but Lily was already opening him up to a whole new world of possibilities in the short time they had known each other. *She is truly magnificent*, he marveled.

Noah decided now might be a good chance to share some of what he had read. "Speaking of the city, I've been reading up on Virginia since we last spoke. It seems Richmond has the largest population in the state. It's also the state capitol. Have you ever been there?"

Lily smiled at Noah's effort, "Oh my, you have been doing your homework. Unfortunately, I've never been to Richmond. My father worked in Norfolk, which is also a large city, so I've been there. It's fun to visit once in a while, but I feel most at home collecting shells by the sea."

"So that's what you were doing!" Noah exclaimed.

"Pardon?"

"The first day I saw you. Well, I suppose you didn't know I was watching you, but I saw you walking about the shore putting something in your basket. It must have been shells?"

Lily brightened, "Oh yes, I was collecting some of the prettiest shells I've ever seen in my life. Have you never taken some for yourself?"

Noah looked down, "No, I'm afraid not. As I've mentioned, I have never been down to the shore."

Lily blushed with embarrassment at her blunder, "Oh yes, I am sorry, I must have forgotten. See, I am a very silly girl. I hope you will forgive me."

Noah didn't want to dwell on the topic, as his attempt to impress Lily with his knowledge of Virginia had been a bust. Instead, he became anxious to show Lily his artwork. He felt confident in his skill, but so much hinged on his ability to impress her where his painting was concerned. He had so little to offer in the way of accomplishments, he didn't want to blow it again. In fact, he had never been nervous quite like this. By comparison, even his art tutor didn't intimidate him, but suddenly the opinion of one person was undermining his confidence. Just the same, it was a major part of himself and he wanted to share his passion for painting with his new friend.

Afraid of how best to broach the topic without appearing too haughty, to his great relief Lily raised the topic first. She too was eager to change course, when she spotted Noah's easel sitting near the window, facing away from them.

"Is that a painting you're working on?" she inquired as she stepped toward it.

"Actually, yes," he said, relieved that she was the one to ask, "But it's not finished. I'd love to show you some of my completed works if you're interested. I have a strong sense that you have an appreciation for good art. I would love your advice."

Lily clapped her hands in front of her and squealed with delight as a young toddler might who had been handed an ice cream cone. "Oh yes, I would love to see your work!" She declared. Her enthusiasm to see his paintings amused Noah greatly and gave him the boost of confidence he needed.

Noah bravely took her by the hand and led her to a

large storage closet just off the sitting-room. He switched on the light to reveal a couple dozen or so painted canvases. Lily's eyes went right to a painting of the sea. The water was dark with rich hues of green and blue among the large cresting foamy waves. The clouds in the distance were dark and ominous—it was the painting he was working on the day of the storm and one he was quite proud of.

"This is utterly beautiful!" Lily said in astonishment. "Did you really paint this yourself?" Noah reddened at the compliment but nodded, "I can feel every part of this," she continued, "as though I have lived this moment myself."

"You did," Noah said proudly, "At least, in part. I did most of the work on this painting the day we met. You almost got washed away." They both laughed as they recalled the rain that interrupted their first interaction.

"It's incredible how well you captured it," was her response as she took a final look.

Lily then turned her attention to the other paintings. Another caught her eye that was bright yellow and green. It was a painting of Aunt Prissy's daffodils. She was then drawn to a fantastic scene of a brooding, grey castle perched on a cliff of an island, overlooking the ocean, surrounded by blue, purple, and pink clouds brightly encircling the castle, casting a colorful light on its surface. Surely, he didn't paint this from real life.

"What was your inspiration for this?" She asked.

"I was thumbing through a book of old English castles before bed one night and dreamed something like it, only the clouds were rolling rapidly around the castle as if to engulf it. I couldn't shake the imagery from my mind, so I had to paint it. The castle seemed to represent a kingdom that had gone dark from isolation, but the colorful, swirling clouds were like some form of magic sent to bring it back to life."

Lily was amazed by the depth and talent of this young man. She considered painting one of her favorite pastimes as well, which she mentioned off-handedly, but Noah's skill was undoubtedly far superior to her own—or anyone else she had ever met. She never considered herself a great artist to begin with, but to her surprise, seeing Noah's work made Lily feel a bit self-conscious about sharing her own. Ultimately, she figured it was enough that they shared a love for painting and so if they were to be friends, she would show him eventually anyway. *Art is not just about skill, but heart,* she told herself, and he had plenty of that too. Lily was now convinced that Noah was much brighter than he let on.

After sharing a few more paintings with Lily, the afternoon sun had begun to make the room feel a bit warm and stuffy, so Noah asked if she would like to step out on the terrace for a bit of fresh air. The sun was indeed high in the sky, causing the water to sparkle like diamonds on the sea. Lily sighed at the breathtaking sight.

"This is quite an amazing view, no wonder you're inspired to paint as you do!" Lily said.

Noah was glad to find her so taken with both his artwork and the view, "Yes, I do enjoy my time out here and find a great deal of inspiration in it. You said that you like to paint as well. Perhaps you might join me some afternoon?" he looked at her, hoping she would like the suggestion.

Lily nodded enthusiastically to affirm her interest in doing so. "I'm definitely not as good as you but as long as you don't tease me, I'd really enjoying painting with you sometime."

Noah couldn't imagine being disappointed in anything Lily did. In his eyes she was more perfect each time he saw her. He was just thrilled to find someone to share his interest with. How did he ever get so lucky to meet such a girl, he wondered?

She walked over to the perfectly manicured shrubbery on the edge of the property and continued looking out to sea. A sailboat in the distance graced the horizon with its white sails, a sight that never failed to strike Noah's heart with melancholy as he imagined his own father to be out there somewhere. He longed to know the freedom of being at sea, the wind whipping through his hair without care or concern. One day, perhaps he too would be brave enough to face the vast ocean.

He followed Lily to the hedge and stood beside her, joining her gaze at the vista before them. They were quiet for a moment, simply content to listen to the roar of the waves together. They were both lulled at once by its hypnotic powers. Finally, Noah broke from the reverie and looked over at Lily to watch her face as she continued gazing outward. She didn't turn her eyes to meet his but continued looking straight ahead, her lips curled slightly upward in delight at the scene before her as tears danced in her wind-swept eyes. *She is a beauty*, he thought, *in the truest sense of the word.*

CHAPTER FIVE

O ver the next month, Noah and Lily saw quite a lot of each other. Lily stopped by most afternoons to spend time talking and painting with Noah. She had summoned the courage to share some of her artwork, to which Noah offered high praise and helpful critique. Even as they painted, he would often break from his own work in progress to demonstrate techniques that would improve the scene she was working on. With Noah's help, Lily was beginning to perceive a noticeable development in her skills. More so than with the help of any teacher she had previously.

Art is where Noah shined. He became like another person—older, wiser, more confident. Sometimes he was a bit tough on her, quick to point out a bad habit she developed and then show her a more effective method. Yet she never took offense and would always respond by saying, "Thank you for your help," as she knew his intentions were only to encourage her growth.

Some days, Lily would walk along the coastline with her white basket collecting seashells or play in the surf and Noah would watch her from his terrace as he painted alone. Both were equally pleasurable to him as he enjoyed observing Lily from a distance as she laughed and romped through the waves as much as he did spending one on one time together. Those moments inspired him to begin work on a new painting of her standing on the shore, which he planned to surprise her with once it was completed.

Lily would often try to gently coax Noah to come out and swim with her or take a walk with her in the woods, but he knew Aunt Prissy would not approve since he was still quite vulnerable to sickness, even in the August heat. The sunshine from sitting on the terrace did him good, but the lack of physical activity made him weak and easily tired out. He determined in his mind to start working on gaining strength and started by taking more strolls in the yard among Aunt Prissy's gardens.

It was fear that ultimately gripped him though. He

had been coddled and sheltered so long he wasn't sure if he could find a place in the outside world. His prison had been comfortable, though enabling. Not that he would ever want to admit it out loud, as it was easier to place the blame on his aunt. Her being so adamant in keeping him home made it all too convenient to never take responsibility for his own lack of fortitude. He accepted his fate without resistance, and it soon became clear that Lily was increasingly aware of his part in the circumstance.

This led to arguments in which Lily would attempt to provoke Noah by pointing out his lack of initiative. She wanted to be patient, but sometimes her frustration got the best of her and Lily would call him out directly, then turn and leave for home until the next day when she would return and apologize for her hurtful words. Noah was easily wounded by Lily's outbursts and hesitated to forgive her, but then she would put her arms around him and beg for his forgiveness, which would melt his stubbornness away.

Noah had outbursts of his own. He didn't like when Lily was late for their afternoon get-togethers and would sometimes make snide remarks for having to wait for her to arrive, which always put her on the defense since being the free spirit that she was, she naturally struggled with being on time. He also revealed his tendency for temper tantrums when he couldn't find some painting tool or supply he was looking for or had run out of and Aunt Prissy didn't have it promptly replaced. His bratty fits were off-putting to Lily, but she dealt with it by not entertaining his mood swings and soon he would calm down, apologize for his unwarranted behavior, and the afternoon would resume as normal.

Noah was ashamed of himself in truth. He never wanted Lily to see this side of him, but they spent so much time together these days, he found it difficult to restrain his behavior on every occasion. These were traits he never thought much about until he met Lily, but now he saw the ugliness of his immature demands. His only consolation was that Lily was inspiring him to be stronger and work toward improvement, so in time, he hoped that he would also overcome his tendency toward anger, fear, and trepidation.

One area he was already noticing a marked improvement was in his newfound interest in learning. In his private time, he was reading more than ever in his life, and not just the usual swashbuckling adventures he so enjoyed, but books on history, science, geography, and philosophy. His appetite for learning was growing and he now found himself looking forward to the upcoming school year. Lily loved discussing all these topics which kept him on his toes. She was so smart, and he was so ignorant; a status he planned to rectify.

As his hunger for knowledge grew, Noah was excessively pleased whenever he could impress Lily with some fact he learned that she didn't already know. She was never sore about it either, but rather encouraged his self-education and was excited to hear all that he had discovered.

Though he was still but a boy in many ways, Noah also began to think more about what it meant to be a man. Lily was certainly the strongest person he knew, yet she also exhibited a sort of vulnerability that called out to the deepest parts of his masculinity. He would watch her in the distance while his heart swelled with affection and he found himself wanting nothing more than to protect her. *What does that mean?* He wondered. *Isn't she the one who is helping me?* He wasn't completely sure if these feelings weren't a typical result of friendship, as he had so little experience with it, but deep down he suspected something more significant was taking place.

Best of all was that Lily seemed to enjoy his company almost as much. She never needed to be convinced to spend time with Noah, came over of her own free will, often bringing him fresh baked cookies and unique seashells she found on the beach.

Even Aunt Prissy was coming around and began to accept Lily's presence in Noah's life. He suspected Prissy even began enjoying her visits as they would often chat a bit and Lily would bring her homemade goodies as well. She remarked more than once that Lily's friendship had turned out to be a good thing for Noah after all and that she was relieved he had not suffered any ill effects because of it. "Sometimes even an old lady like myself can be proven wrong," she boasted in false humility. "And I'm not one who will refuse to say it."

This made Noah glad, but even with all the pleasant distractions Lily offered, one thing still loomed large in the back of his young mind—Noah's father would soon be home. Fishing season usually wrapped up in September and for once Noah had exciting things to share with his father, not just the other way around. Noah decided he would also ask his father to teach him more about the fishing trade. Noah had never considered a career but was now developing an interest in understanding his father's trade to see how it suited him. He began daydreaming about going out to sea and fishing alongside him, hauling in lobster crates and working on ship repairs together in the winter. Perhaps a real relationship with his father was still possible.

But a month was still a long way off and Noah wanted to enjoy the rest of the summer by simply appreciating the joy he found in his time with Lily. It was the thing that made him get up every morning and face each new day. Aside from his father, he thought of little else, or at least little else that didn't somehow have a connection to his friendship with Lily.

CHAPTER SIX

Noah was preparing for Lily's afternoon visit when a letter from his father arrived. He had just put out his easel and brushes when Aunt Prissy came rushing into the room, breathless with excitement over hearing from her brother, Martin, for the first time in two months.

"It came," she called out, waving the letter over her head, "It finally came! Word from your father. We must read this at once!"

Noah did his best to appear nonchalant, but inwardly he was just as anxious to hear from his father as Aunt Prissy was. "Go on, Aunt Prissy," he said while setting down a palette next to his brushes, "Read it out loud." Aunt Prissy pulled the letter out, her hands shaking, and began to read.

Dear Noah and Priss,

I hope this letter finds you both well. It has been a particularly busy season. I've been spending many long days at sea with a surly crew, working hard to fulfill orders. Along with that, there are fewer handymen about than last year, so I've been picking up odd jobs fixing up people's boats and equipment. I can't really say the reason for this, but since there is such a great opportunity for me to make some extra money as the season slows down, you should not expect me next month as I'll be staying a bit longer than usual. I know what a great disappointment this must be for you both, so to make it up to you I am sending additional funds for the month and have included a special early birthday gift for Noah. I planned to give him this on his eighteenth birthday, but since he's been the man of the house for a while now, I thought he should have it. Tell Noah to take good care of it, keep it wound and polished and it should last him a long time. Take care of each other.

Aunt Prissy reached into the envelope and pulled something out wrapped in tissue paper. She unfolded it to reveal a wad of cash and beneath it, Martin's gold pocket watch. Noah stared in disbelief as she handed it to him.

"My father's watch, I can't believe it," he whispered in awe, wanting to be upset about the news but too surprised by the extravagant gift. "I have never known father to be without it. I always hoped one day he'd give it to me, but I didn't expect it so soon."

"Well, it's simply too much if you ask me, Noah," Aunt Prissy began, "It's not exactly the kind of gift you give a young boy, and you, not even seventeen yet. Why would he go and do an impetuous thing like that? Now, what will he use to tell time?"

Noah didn't respond immediately, but instead turned the watch over in his hand, admiring its intricate beauty. "My mother gave him this for a wedding present," he answered finally, "I can think of no better present on earth."

Aunt Prissy sighed with defeat, "Well, I'm sure it's just fine. How much damage could be done to it after all? You will keep it safely indoors at all times, of course, as long as your father isn't here to oversee things."

Noah laughed bitterly. "Which means it should never leave the house! And where else would I take it? It's not as if I ever step foot from Birchwood Cottage anyway."

Aunt Prissy sat upright with a look of indignation. "Now listen here my dear boy, don't you get smart. You know very well it is for your own good that I keep you home as I do. Maybe one day when you're strong and healthy you can think about venturing out into the world. That is, with your father's blessing, of course. But for now, this is where you stay as long as I am keeping watch over you. And if that fool girl tries to put any ideas in your head, she's got another thing coming. In fact, perhaps I'll put an end to the visits altogether. The last thing I need is further aggravation while your dear father is away."

Noah didn't respond further. He was greatly unhappy with Aunt Prissy's threat and was tempted to strike back but didn't feel it was worth the fight with Lily stopping by shortly. Until then he just wanted to reflect on his father's disheartening news and spend time polishing up the old watch.

Aunt Prissy took his silence as a victory and softened slightly. "Now be a good boy and put this watch away before Lily gets here. No use inviting trouble. No matter how much you think you know a person you never can tell who's eyeing what you got and wanting it for themselves."

Noah was visibly annoyed by her comments but set the pocket watch in the drawer on the end table so as to appease his aunt in hopes she would leave his room. To his great relief, she seemed satisfied with the gesture and exited, leaving Noah to his thoughts.

Forty-five minutes later there was a knock at the sitting-room door. Lily entered to the sound of Noah calling out, "Come in," as he always did. She found him standing at his easel with his back turned to her. He was in deep concentration as he painted furiously upon the canvas before him. She approached him softly, not wanting to disturb his concentration.

Noah often found he could think best when he painted. It was as though his body would take over the physical act of painting as he turned things over in his mind. Right now, he was working on a vase of red daylilies picked from Aunt Prissy's garden. Swiftly he painted streaks of crimson and gold, with great fervor and intensity. It appeared as though they were on fire. Lily watched with rapt attention, mesmerized by his depth and skill. Her breathing quickened with every stroke. He was like a maestro working the bow of the violin in Vivaldi's Summer. Who was this genius before her?

And like that, his mad concerto came to a halt and a masterpiece in the making set before him; one single daylily, larger than life with an expression of both passion and affliction. He set down his brush and looked up in a daze as if noticing Lily had arrived for the first time. "Hello," he greeted her softly. "Sorry I was just working on this piece and I guess I got caught up in the moment."

Lily smiled, her eyes shining with tears, "Please don't apologize. Watching you just now was magnificent, Noah. You have an amazing gift."

Noah blushed, "Thank you for your kindness, Lily, would you like to join me?"

Lily grabbed the satchel holding her brushes then looked around, "No terrace today?"

"No, it's a bit chilly today so Aunt Prissy thought I should paint inside."

Lily scrunched her face in confusion. "What do you mean? It's a little breezy, but quite warm out."

Noah simply shrugged his shoulders and Lily took a seat beside him, feeling irked once again over Aunt Prissy's shielding and Noah's willingness to just go along with whatever silly thing she told him. She weighed whether to press the issue but thought better of it as she didn't want to ruin the beauty of the moment. She sat down and set to work on a field of daisies she had started earlier that week.

Noah leaned over to take a look. "It's coming together nicely. Perhaps add a little darker green in some spots in the grass for greater dimension. That will really stand out."

Lily dipped the tip of her brush in the black and swirled it with a medium green paint until she got the desired hue. Once again, Noah was right. The field looked more brilliant as she worked in the darker green.

Noah went back to work on his own canvas when he casually said, "I heard from my father today."

"Oh?"

"Turns out he won't be here next month after all. I was hoping you could meet him."

Lily could hear the pain in Noah's voice and felt sad for his disappointing news, "I'm so sorry Noah," she said placing a hand on his arm. "I'm sure he wishes he could be here too."

Noah shook his head. "I don't think so. His seasons get longer every year and his time spent at home gets shorter before he has to run back for one thing or another. I remember as a boy when we would spend seven months out of the year together straight, but that was a long time ago. And Aunt Prissy just makes excuses for him. What's worse is that she always wants to put things off until he is here to get his approval, but that time is so limited now."

Noah then read her the entire letter, showed her the gold pocket watch he gave him, and filled her in on more of the conversation he had with his aunt that afternoon. Lily listened quietly to Noah, only interrupting to ask the occasional question for clarification. He was getting more emotional by the minute, the more he talked of his father's absence and his aunt's controlling ways. Lily's heart went out to him but more than anything she wished to move him to action.

"Noah, your father referred to you as the man of the house. Did you ever think that maybe it's time to start acting like it?"

Noah was immediately defensive. "What do you mean by that?" he shot back.

Lily paused then tried again, "Sorry, it's not the way it sounded. I just mean maybe it's time to take control of your own destiny and stop allowing Aunt Prissy to dictate your every move. Show her that you are not the weak, feeble boy she makes you out to be. I know you are stronger than that and once you step out and take some risks there will be no going back. She's going to have to live with your newfound freedom."

Noah put his hand up to quiet Lily down, "Please stop talking like that Lily, if my aunt hears you she'll ask you to leave and never return. In fact, she said as much this afternoon."

Lily didn't lower her voice even slightly, "No, I won't stop Noah. You need to hear that you are capable of more than what she's allowing you to do...what you are allowing yourself to do. You need to get out of this house, for your own good! Think about it Noah, what fun we could have. Don't you want to go down to the sea with me and take walks through the woods? Don't you want to go to the market and watch the boats coming into port? Oh Noah, don't you see what you're missing out on being cooped up here...what we're missing out on together?"

Noah was hearing none of it, "Look Lily, it's been a very difficult day for me. Can we just not do this right now? I don't know if I have much energy left and I don't want to cause further issues with Aunt Prissy. I really just need you both to leave me alone right now."

Lily was taken aback by that final statement, "Are you asking me to go home then?"

Noah stopped Lily from standing up, "No, no, I just don't want to have this discussion right now. You knew when we became friends what my circumstance is, and I thought you understood."

"I've tried my best to understand, but the thing is, I can't help but see how much more you're capable of. How can I be a real friend and never encourage you to do better for yourself? It's just not healthy, Noah."

It was all Noah could take and he finally snapped at Lily, "That's enough! If you want to keep having this conversation, then I am going to have to ask you to leave. Aunt Prissy is only trying to do what's best for me and if she says I'm not ready, then I have to trust her. I needed your friendship today, but I can see that was too much to ask."

Lily could see she wasn't getting anywhere, and that Noah was being overemotional. She didn't mean to get him worked up, especially with the news he received concerning his father's delayed return home. She decided to apologize and drop the subject, but deep down her frustration was building and she didn't know how long she could bite her tongue before bringing up the topic once again.

CHAPTER SEVEN

L ily was growing restless. While she did indeed enjoy her time with Noah immensely, she was becoming increasingly frustrated by his lack of mobility and his own role in being perpetually homebound. Aunt Prissy may have been the one who initiated his imprisonment, but he was doing nothing to make a break for it. Lily was a free spirit and one who loved to seek after little adventures, and though quite independent in doing so, she often mourned that she had no companion to join her on occasion. She wanted that person to be Noah, but he had left her feeling disappointed once again.

Her desire to get Noah to move beyond the

restrictions of Birchwood Cottage's perimeter was not totally selfish either. She also thought about how beneficial it would be for Noah to partake in the fun rather than just hearing about her experiences. Sure, he never begrudged her the joy of going out. In fact, he always listened with keen interest about the places she went, showing enthusiasm in general, but she also sensed a bit of sadness overcame him as well at not being able to experience it for himself. She really couldn't help but pity him for missing out on the many rocky ocean vistas he could paint, exploring the sea caves, studying the aquatic creatures and plants in the tide pools, seeing the little woodland animals grazing about in the early morning, or hearing the magic of the wind rustling through the trees on nature hikes. Even taking pleasure in watching the large ships come and go from the channel and the bustle of people buying and selling in the market.

But more than anything, Lily pitied him for never feeling the sand between his toes or knowing the exhilaration of jumping though the powerful waves of the sea and feeling the saltwater on his bare skin. How could one live at the ocean's door and never enter? There was no greater thrill on earth as far as Lily was concerned and she made every attempt to get him to try, but so far, she had failed miserably. She was no longer hopeful that he would one day make a breakthrough, which did not bode well for their friendship long-term.

Lily was sitting on her old beach quilt contemplating all these things when she heard the sound of voices approaching from the north end of the beach, past the blue cottage. She looked up and saw a small, cheerful family heading toward the shoreline which included a mom, dad, a brother, and sister. The brother appeared to be the older of the two, though they both looked close to her age, more or less.

The girl was petite with a head of raven black, shoulder-length hair adorned with spiral curls that bounced when she walked. The boy had dark hair as well which was long on top and fell across his brow. He had a tan complexion, unusual for people in the north, most likely from spending a lot of time in the sun. Lily wanted to get a closer look at these sudden visitors but decided to wait until they approached. They seemed to take notice of Lily sitting peacefully by herself, so she waved a friendly hello. They waved back, the young girl showing more enthusiasm than the rest, and proceeded to set up a small picnic lunch.

Lily continued watching them with great interest as she did not recognize the family and so few people came to this spot for swimming. She then remembered a couple of weeks ago hearing her parents mention offhandedly that a cottage two houses down had been bought by a family that would be moving in soon. She wondered if this might be that very family. She wanted to go and introduce herself but didn't want to interrupt their time together as they were in the middle of enjoying their lunch.

Instead, Lily decided to head back to the water for a little swim. She waded contentedly in the surf for quite some time when she noticed the boy and girl had finished their lunch and were heading for the water as well. The boy was carrying a wooden board and Lily watched with fascination as he rushed into the waves without hesitation, hugging it close to his body. She had seen people in Virginia use similar wooden boards to ride on waves and always thought it looked like great fun the way it would carry them swiftly to the shore.

The girl was quick to take to the sea as well. Clearly, they were both accustomed to it. She very much enjoyed splashing against the waves and screamed playfully as they crested over her tiny frame. Lily wondered how she might go about approaching the brother and sister, but soon the young girl waded into her vicinity to introduce herself.

"Hi there! My name's Flora Durgin, what's your name?" she smiled brightly when their eyes met.

Lily was glad the girl spoke first and appeared to be as friendly and outgoing as herself. "My name is Lily Stephens," she answered. "Are you the new family that recently moved in?"

"Yup, we sure are! We arrived just a couple of days ago, and I've been aching to go down to the beach ever since we got here. It's great fun, don't you think?"

Lily nodded in agreement, "It sure is! I only recently moved here myself, from Virginia. The water is a bit colder up north but otherwise, it's divine. Where did you move here from?"

Flora dipped her head under the water and then came back up before answering, "Oh, we've always lived in Maine, but closer to the city. Dad thought it would be nice to buy a house a little further out on the shore and this house came up for sale. That's my mom and dad right there," she pointed to the happy couple still sitting on the picnic blanket. They waved back and continued their conversation, "and that's my brother Everett. He's a couple of years older than me."

Just then Flora's brother made his way through the surf to join the two young girls. Flora didn't pause to introduce him and instead added, "Everett isn't as excited to be here as I am. He was upset about moving because he had to leave his girl." She rolled her eyes and made a face that indicated to Lily that Flora did not care too much for the girl.

"What are you saying about me, you little rascal?" Flora's brother, Everett, demanded playfully.

"I was just telling my new friend here about your boring girl back home and how you won't stop crying over her."

"Hey, Julie wasn't boring. And she wasn't my girl. She was just a friend."

"Yeah, a boring friend." Flora turned to Lily, "She never liked to have any fun. She was so stuck-up."

Everett laughed. "You were just jealous because she had prettier dresses than you." Flora stuck her tongue out at Everett in reply, but he just smiled. "And don't harass this poor lady. She doesn't know what a little monster you can be yet."

He then proceeded to dunk his sister underwater and gave Lily a lopsided grin. He was quite a nice-looking boy with a strong build and dark eyes that danced with mischief.

Flora pushed back at her brother and dove back under to swim. Clearly, this was their own playful way of interacting and no feelings seemed hurt on either end. Both Flora and Everett seemed like fun-loving kids and Lily was eager to get to know them better.

"Well, it looks like you know my name, what's yours?" Everett asked in order to keep the conversation going.

"Lily Stephens. I was telling your sister I moved here from Virginia a little over a month ago. She said you are the new family that just moved in. It's great to meet you both!"

"Yes, well, what she said is true. I did have a difficult time with the move, but it wasn't just because of some girl. We grew up in that house and it wasn't easy to leave all my friends behind. I must say though, it sure is nice to meet someone so soon! What do you do around here for fun?"

Lily thought about it for a minute. "Not much to be honest. The beach has been my favorite spot to spend the day. There is a nice patch of woods near here with some pretty trails to walk along. I go there often."

"Wow, that sounds great! You'll have to tell me all about them."

"Well, you and your sister could join me for a walk sometime if you'd like."

Everett gave her another one of his lopsided grins, "We'll definitely take you up on that offer!"

Lily felt her tummy get a little lopsided as well. Perhaps now she would actually have friends to do some fun things with.

CHAPTER EIGHT

L ittle did Lily know that in the distance Noah was watching her interaction with Flora and Everett from the terrace. He was curious as to who these new visitors were and was becoming increasingly anxious as he observed the exuberant nature of their conversation. He wanted to continue working on his painting of the daylilies but was having a difficult time concentrating. He suddenly felt ill under the hot summer sun and thought he might go lie down for a bit.

As he packed up his painting tools, he kept his eye on the group of new friends the whole time. Lily's sparkling laughter carried on the sea breeze and the boy she was with handed her a wooden board that she laid on top of. The boy proceeded to help Lily steady herself on the board so that when a big wave came rolling up, she lunged herself on top of it just before it crested which caused her to rush to the coastline until she tumbled into the surf. She got up, soaked and laughing, and headed back to try again. The boy was applauding while the young girl jumped up and down splashing the water in celebration of Lily's ride on a wave.

Noah wondered why he suddenly felt so queasy. He was fine this morning but now he was feeling sick to his stomach. Perhaps Aunt Prissy was right in warning him that he was still susceptible to sickness in the summer. He folded his easel, grabbed his canvas gently, along with the paints and brushes, then headed into the cool cottage to rest.

When he got to his bedroom he laid down on the bed and attempted to fall asleep, but his brain was reeling with so many thoughts and questions. Who were those people? How did Lily know them? Why was she laughing so much? She sure looked like she was having more fun with them than she ever had with him. Would Lily stop by tomorrow as usual? Perhaps he would get some answers then.

Just then he heard a knock coming from the entrance door so he sat up, wondering if it might be Lily. Once he could make out the voices speaking it sounded like Reverend Thomas so he assumed he and his family must have stopped by to check in on them. They hadn't been by in quite some time, so it seemed they were due for a visit.

Aunt Prissy knocked on Noah's bedroom door and asked if he would come and greet the Reverend. Noah still didn't feel very well, but he straightened himself out and went into the hall. Reverend Thomas smiled and greeted Noah warmly as he entered. There was no sign of Mrs. Thomas, but Ruth and Leah were standing quietly beside their father, donned in their Sunday best, even though it was only Wednesday.

He noticed Ruth was wearing what appeared to be a new dress that was more fashionable than her usual plain frocks. Her red hair was pinned up in curls and he even spotted a bit of blush on her cheeks. Noah never considered Ruth to be very attractive, but this new look was quite becoming. In fact, the more he gazed upon her he had to admit to himself that she actually looked very pretty. Not at all the dour girl he was used to seeing. If Leah had an opinion about Ruth's recent transformation it didn't show. She was her usual timid self, staring at the floor and twirling her unkempt auburn locks.

Reverend Thomas was prattling away about his latest

sermon, the recent charity causes run by Mrs. Thomas, and how his dear wife was out of town visiting her poor ailing mother. Aunt Prissy politely listened while Noah stood there silently, his mind wandering back to his former troubling thoughts. Ruth approached him with an unusually toothy grin and asked how he was enjoying his summer.

Noah was surprised to hear the girl speak up in such a bold fashion, as she rarely spoke at all. It occurred to him that he had said very few words to Ruth himself, despite the fact that she had visited on a regular basis for as long as he could remember. "It's been alright," he replied. "I've been focusing a lot on my painting." He hesitated and for fear of appearing rude added, "How about yours?"

Ruth batted her eyes in reply, "It's been just splendid. I stayed with my dear grandmother for a time before she fell ill. She lives in Portland which is a lovely city. We did a great deal of shopping and had tea every afternoon. She's a proper English woman, you know. Even after living in Maine for fifty years she still has her accent. Now we're not sure if she'll pull through. I'm quite devastated at the thought."

"I'm sorry to hear that," Noah said sincerely, musing how he had never heard Ruth talk so freely. She seemed to now take after her father who was still going on at a similar rate with Aunt Prissy. Ruth continued speaking about her time in Portland and Noah's mind began drifting back to Lily and the boy she was with in the water. His thoughts were suddenly interrupted when he realized Ruth had asked him a question.

"I'm sorry, what did you ask?" he inquired, blushing slightly.

"England. Would you like to visit someday?"

Noah brushed a hand through his hair as he considered the question. "To be honest, I've never much thought of it, but I guess I would. I love looking through my book of old English castles and I suppose it would be nice to see them in person someday."

Ruth seemed pleased that he shared her interest in England. "Well, perhaps one day when we're all grown, we'll run into each other there and recall how we used to know each other as kids." She giggled like a girl and it surprised Noah how kitten-like her behavior was.

Leah continued to seem disinterested in anything that was being said. It was as if she was in her own little world. Ruth caught Noah staring at her sister and said, "Oh don't worry about her. She doesn't mean anything by it. Her odd behavior, that is. She has been this way since she was little. Never very talkative or affectionate. My parents took her to see a doctor, you know. They aren't exactly sure what's wrong, but it seems to be mental."

Noah had never heard his aunt speak of Leah having any mental issues. It explained a lot, but it was curious none the less. "Is she unhappy?" he asked.

"I don't think so. Leah stays in her own head most of the time. She seems content as long as we don't try to force her to do things she doesn't like, such as playing in the sand or eating certain foods."

"Does she ever talk to you about it?"

Ruth glanced over at her sister who seemed oblivious to their conversation. "No, she speaks sometimes but we don't really have conversations. It used to make me sad but now I'm used to it. In some ways, I'm an only child like you, Noah."

Noah never thought that he and Ruth would have much in common. He always assumed Ruth and Leah were similar. They both always had that blank, sad stare but apparently, Ruth's came from loneliness. She was more alive now than he had ever seen her—friendly even. Noah began to consider that perhaps he had misjudged them both. It didn't seem to be Leah's fault for the way she was either. He now felt sorry for the mean things he thought and decided to see if he had any books that might help him understand what kind of mental issues Leah suffered from.

The Reverend had just finished his attempt to impress upon Aunt Prissy some spiritual insights he amassed from a recent book he was studying on the life of John Wesley when he saw Noah and Ruth in conversation. He called to his daughter, letting her know it was about time to go but not before inviting Noah to church sometime. "You know, the Lord's house is always open to you, young man."

Aunt Prissy quickly interjected, "Oh Reverend, it's much appreciated but Noah here doesn't leave the house as you know, for he is quite sickly and can't take the risk of catching pneumonia."

"Nonsense Priscilla," the Reverend blustered. "Why, if that young man is ailing there is no better place for him to be! We pray for you both often and hope you'll soon grace us with your presence, my dear." Reverend Thomas then stood up, gathered his daughters, and headed for the door. Ruth waved sadly to Noah as the door closed behind her.

Noah was more confused than ever. In all the time he had known the Thomas's he could not recall so strange a visit, as if they weren't unusual enough to begin with. He had never thought much of going to church or God, but the invitation was surprising and intriguing. Perhaps this was another thing he'd have to add to his list of new things to try. He'd talk it over with Lily tomorrow—that is, if she was still coming.

CHAPTER NINE

Lily was having such fun with Everett and Flora the next morning that she almost forgot about her visit with Noah. She had taken them to the trail in the woods as promised and they were enjoying themselves so very much observing the frantic activities of the chipmunks and squirrels and hiding from each other behind the large old maple trees. Everett was proving to be quite a mischievous imp. He would pull his sister's curly pigtails and then run away quickly. He was so very fast, and she could never catch him with her short legs, so she'd scream instead that one day she would get him back for all his mean tricks. Of course, she didn't mean it at all. She loved her older brother and enjoyed his teasing.

He even began teasing Lily a little, but not in a mean way. Sometimes he would snatch the wildflower she picked out of her hand and hold it high above her head so she couldn't grab it, then give it back when she gave up, or punch her playfully in the arm when she wouldn't laugh at his corny jokes. She actually did find them quite amusing, but she liked making him work for her attention.

Everett was so different from Noah. He was strong and fast. He could climb a tree swiftly like a monkey or swim in the sea with agility like a dolphin. He was loud and funny, good-natured, and playful. Noah possessed many good qualities too. He was always gentle and kind, sweet, thoughtful, and considerate. He treated Lily like she was a porcelain doll, doting on her and praising her efforts when she improved her painting skills. He was smart too and she enjoyed their conversations as his interest in learning increased. She truly did take great pleasure in their afternoons together but having someone to romp with was nice for a change.

Flora had her own endearing traits as well. She was cute and bubbly and took to Lily right away, like a little sister. She was always eager to see what pretty shells Lily found or cheer her on when she caught a wave on Everett's board. She also had some neat interests of her own. Flora loved making colorful beaded necklaces and was learning to play the piano. She promised to play for Lily sometime if she ever wanted to come over for a visit. Lily was thankful for these new playmates.

It was just after one o'clock when Lily realized she was over an hour late for her visit with Noah. The threesome was just about at the end of the trail heading out of the woods when it dawned on her that she completely lost track of time. She turned suddenly to her new friends and apologized for leaving in such a hurry but that she had to go. She was off like a shot before they could even respond and were left bewildered by her sudden departure.

"Will we see you again soon?" Everett called out to her.

"Yes, I'll be around!" She called back in return before disappearing around the trail.

Lily ran out of the trees and onto the beach for a direct shot to Noah's house. She removed her shoes so she could move swiftly through the warm sand. When she arrived at Noah's house she looked up and was hoping to see him on the terrace lost in one of his paintings, but there was no sign of him. She ran up the grassy hill to the front of the house and approached his doorway, knocking breathlessly. When Aunt

Prissy opened the door, Lily was flushed and panting.

"Hi, I'm here to see Noah!" She panted between breaths.

"A little later than usual, aren't you dear? He's in his sitting-room, go ahead…"

Lily didn't let Prissy finish before rushing past her. She entered the sitting-room without even knocking and found Noah standing by the window looking out at the sea. He didn't turn around right away, even though he knew she was standing there. He waited for her to speak.

"I'm so sorry I'm late Noah," Lily said adding an upbeat inflection to her tone, "I was out in the woods and lost track of time."

Noah turned around to face her and could see she had been running. Her cheeks were still rosy, her hair a bit disheveled and she had yet to find a moment to put her shoes back on. "I was afraid you might not come today," came his flat reply.

Lily looked down and shuffled her feet a bit. "Of course I would come. I said I would, didn't I?"

Noah was still feeling hurt, as he had begun to accept that she wouldn't show up but decided to let Lily off the hook for being late since she came after all. "Well, I'm glad you're here now anyway. Tell me, what else have you been up to?"

"Oh, just the usual…" Lily trailed, unsure of why she didn't want to tell Noah about Everett and Flora. She originally intended to but now she felt uncomfortable about it.

Noah pressed. "I saw you were talking to some new people on the beach the other day. Who are they?"

Now Lily wished she had just mentioned it since he already seemed to know. "Oh yeah, that's the new family that just moved on our street. They live a couple of houses down from me. They are very nice."

Noah's spirits fell with the realization that these were permanent residents. He swallowed hard. "Oh, do you think they will be your new friends now?"

"Yes, I think they are quite nice, and I would like them to be friends." Lily shifted.

"And you'll forget all about me I suppose?"

"No, of course not. Why would say that, Noah?"

Noah's eyes flashed with spite, "Well, I'm sure you'd much rather have friends who are fun and are able do things with you outside of these four walls!" His voice was growing louder now.

Lily was taken aback. "Noah, I've only just met Everett and Flora but I'm sure you'd like them too…"

"Oh, so Everett is his name? I don't need any other friends, Lily. I never needed any friends before, why should I need them now?" Noah wasn't exactly sure why his anger was escalating to such a degree, but his emotions were taking over all reason.

"Surely you don't mean that…"

"Yes, I do! Actually, I don't need you either, so why don't you just go hang out with your new exciting friends and leave me alone! I'm sure that's what you were doing anyway before you came here. In fact, I bet you didn't even want to come at all!"

Noah's jealousy had gotten the better of him. His bitter words took Lily by surprise and she became silent for a moment then spat back, "Ya know what, you're absolutely right, I shouldn't have come! All you do is lock yourself up in this dusty old room day after day. You never want to get out of here and I'm sick of it. I want fresh air and it would be good for you too if you weren't such a…coward!" Noah looked crestfallen and Lily knew she went too far but she couldn't take it back now. Instead, she turned on her heel and headed for the door.

"Go ahead and leave, that's just fine with me!" Noah called out as Lily exited the room. He then ran to his bedroom to cry bitterly into his pillow. He had allowed his emotions to get the better of him once again and he wondered how long before Lily wouldn't forgive him one more time, especially now that she had better options of who to spend her time with. He was sure he had blown it this time for good. Her biting words rang in his ears as never before. *Coward.* He wanted to hate her for saying it, most of all because she was right.

CHAPTER TEN

T he next morning Noah woke up with an awful pit in his stomach. He had not slept well the night before and tossed and turned throughout. His head was heavy, and his eyes were swollen from the tears he cried. Lily was his dearest friend, his only friend, and he certainly had chased her off for good this time with his jealous rage. Now he knew what she really thought of him, yet he could not deny the truth of her words. It was time to start acting like a man, but he felt so inadequate.

Noah sluggishly got out of bed and dressed himself before going out to the terrace for some fresh air. When he stepped outside Lily was there waiting for him, a forlorn look on her pretty face. It startled him and he wasn't positive he wasn't still dreaming.

"I'm glad you're awake," she said softly.

"What are you doing here?"

"I came to apologize."

"For what?"

"The harsh things I said. I couldn't sleep at all last night. I had to come over first thing this morning."

Somehow this made Noah feel better about his own sleepless night. "Me either…"

"I really shouldn't have said those things. I know it's difficult for you…"

Noah cut her off. "No, it was all my fault. You didn't deserve to be treated that way. You have been a true friend to me. Lily, you've made my whole world come alive and I suppose I am scared of losing you, but I see that I've only been chasing you away. And you know what, you were right…I am a coward. I know it. My whole life I have lived in the safety of Birchwood Cottage and I don't know if I have the strength to change that. You really do deserve better friends."

"That's not true!" Lily insisted. "You have been nothing but wonderful to me since I've moved here. I value your friendship very much and I believe in you! You have the power to do anything you want—you just have to put your mind to it. You won't do it alone…I'll help you."

"Why would you want to?" Noah looked down in shame.

"Because I want good things for you, Noah. I know in my heart that you are far stronger than you give yourself credit for. You are smart and talented and could do anything you put your mind to. I've seen how quickly you learn when you make the effort. I think you could do the same for your physical wellbeing too. You just need to try. Please."

Lily's soft, pleading eyes struck Noah in his core. He loved Lily, that he could no longer deny. The thought of losing her was more than he could ever bear. Perhaps he could try for her sake. He stepped forward with outstretched arms and was filled with warmth when she fell into them with a firm embrace.

"Maybe I can do it with your help. You're the only one who could make me believe that."

He looked down at Lily's sweet smiling face and wanted to kiss her, but didn't know how, so instead he kissed her forehead and released his grip. "So now what?"

Lily replied. "Well, we don't have to do everything all at once. How about we just have a peaceful afternoon together and do some painting. We can begin tomorrow."

Noah liked that idea and agreed quite heartily with her suggestion. Lily left the house to run home and grab her painting supplies and returned quickly. They spent a beautiful breezy afternoon on the terrace painting, talking, laughing, and sharing thoughts about books they recently read. There was a newly established quiet intimacy between them, having made another breakthrough in their friendship. It was as if they were older suddenly, wiser. It also created a new appreciation for the other's significance in their lives and even Lily felt a special closeness to Noah even more than before. She finally had hope that he would make new strides in overcoming the restrictions that held him back from experiencing a fulfilling life. It meant even more knowing she was part of making that happen.

Feeling invigorated by the happy turn of events, Noah was suddenly struck with an idea "Hey, why not start today after all? Let's take our easels out to the beach grass beyond the hedges. It's not a big step, but it's something we can do together."

No matter how small the gesture, Lily was excited to see Noah taking the initiative to start pushing himself outside of his comfort zone. He took Lily's hand to help her over the row of shrubs first, handed her the easels and paint, then climbed over himself. It really wasn't so scary out there at all.

A daring thought crossed his mind that perhaps it wouldn't be long before he would feel brave enough to face the sea himself. With Lily by his side, anything was possible.

They promptly set their supplies back up and in no time and were peacefully painting once again and chattering along when Aunt Prissy came rushing through the terrace door in a manic state. "Noah, what in heavens are you doing out there on the grass...and with all this wind? Don't you know you could catch your death of cold? This ocean air is not good for you, it will clog your lungs for sure!"

They both turned to Prissy in astonishment at her overreaction to the light breeze. She was all in a panic as she rushed over the hedges to where they were standing. Noah stood up and calmly said, "Aunt, what are you talking about? The wind isn't hurting me. It's actually doing me some good to get fresh air. Please don't worry."

"Don't worry? Are you kidding? Did I not promise your father that I would take care of you and protect you while he is away? This painting will be the death of you yet! You spend too much time out here in the elements as it is, inhaling this paint and turpentine, and now you're venturing out past the terrace. Heaven knows what's next! Why even last night I noticed how you tossed and turned like a boy with a fever. You might be coming down with something. Here, let me check..."

Aunt Prissy reached out to place her hand on Noah's head when he pushed it away and said, "No, Aunt Prissy, I'm perfectly fine! I'm not sick, I was just upset about some things last night, but everything is okay now."

"No, I don't believe you, Noah Sullivan! You can see as well as I can that the weather is beginning to turn and it's time to put an end to these long afternoons out in the elements. Now grab your easel and come inside this instant!"

Noah stood up to protest when Aunt Prissy pushed past him to grab his easel and in the struggle, the canvas knocked over and yellow paint spilled on top of the beautiful sunset he was in the middle of composing. Everyone stopped and was silent for a moment. Lily stood frozen with her mouth gaping open and Noah stood staring at the painting trying to process the loss of his work.

Aunt Prissy broke the unsettling silence with a loud sob. "Look what you made me do! You were always such a good, obedient boy. That is until *she* came along." Her eyes flashed in Lily's direction. "That girl, always filling your head with stuff and nonsense! I told you having friends would be a risk to your health."

"That's not true..." Noah attempted, desperate to interrupt her accusations while Lily stood blushing a crimson red, not having expected to be brought into the argument.

Prissy continued. "It is! And now you don't care if you put your life in danger and make me break my promise to your dear old father. I suppose you don't care if you make him suffer more than he already has. You are a selfish boy, selfish I tell ya! Well, I won't have it."

Lily tried to gently interject to make an appeal on Noah's behalf. "Listen, Prissy," she began. "If you only knew how much better Noah is getting you wouldn't worry so. Surely his father would be glad to see Noah doing so well. You have to believe he would want him to be free to enjoy life and all it offers. And he is becoming stronger now. Don't you see? All this effort to shelter him is actually making him weaker."

That was it for Aunt Prissy. She could no longer endure these claims, so she turned sharply to Lily and began raging, "I knew you were the one filling his head. Listen, girl, Noah was just fine until you came along. If you care about him at all then you need to leave right now. In fact, you are no longer welcome in this house again. Do you hear me?"

Noah jumped in with a desperate cry. "No Aunt Priss! Don't do this, she is good and only means well. Please…"

But Aunt Prissy continued to stand her ground, shouting demands for Lily to leave at once. Lily was so frightened by the terrible passion in the woman's voice that she did not protest further and ran speedily through the tall grass and toward her home, leaving her painting utensils behind her. Noah called after her, but it was too late. Lily was gone.

CHAPTER ELEVEN

Noah cleaned up the mess Aunt Prissy made of his sunset painting and went back inside. She was still in quite a manic state, so he decided to proceed with caution. Surely Lily wouldn't take her words seriously. She would be back, he felt certain of it. Aunt Prissy just had a way of overreacting sometimes but she never meant to hurt anyone. He hoped that maybe once she calmed down she would go next door and apologize to Lily, but the hours passed and that didn't happen.

Later that evening Noah went to the dining hall to have supper with Aunt Prissy and despite having gained some control of her emotions, she was still quite worked up over the incident. He didn't say a word at first, just concentrated on eating his soup, but he couldn't take the uncomfortable silence much longer, so finally, he decided to speak up.

"Aunt Priss, about Lily…"

She quickly interrupted before he could lay the foundation of his case. "I don't want to talk about it. The girl is not welcome here and that's final!"

"How can you say that? You know as well as I do that Lily has been good for me. She is nothing but kind…"

"Oh, you might believe that—she has done a great job of working her feminine charms on you after all—but she is a selfish girl, and I won't have her making you that way. She doesn't care one bit if you get sick and die. I went against my better judgment in allowing her to visit so often. I now see what a mistake it was to do so. Your father will be home soon enough, and he will ensure that my rules are obeyed."

Noah doubted very much his father would care one way or another. A simple request from a brother many years ago, a promise made under great duress, had turned into an obsession for his aunt and he began to suspect that she was not well. Noah thought perhaps she had mental issues like Leah.

"I am looking forward to my father coming home as there are a lot of things we will need to discuss when he gets here. But in the meantime, I am asking that you would please not forbid Lily from coming to visit. At least until he returns. If Father agrees with your concerns, I promise to adhere to them, but in the meantime, I need you to go and make things right with Lily."

Aunt Prissy was unmoved. Her lips tightened as Noah spoke then she retorted with much sourness. "I will do no such thing. That girl is a menace to your health, and I will not have you taking unnecessary risks between now and then. So just forget it, I don't want to hear another word about it."

With that she picked herself up out of the dining chair, her food barely touched, and marched off to her bedroom. That was the last Noah saw of her for the night. Sad and defeated, Noah finished his supper then cleaned up what was left on the table and retired to his own quarters. He was desperate to fix things but didn't know how. No matter how he looked at it, he was still at his aunt's mercy and there was definitely no open door that night to talk about things further. He had never seen her so determined, even against his pleas.

Noah was about to head to bed when the sight of the moon reflecting off the ocean caught his attention from the terrace door. He approached the glass for a closer look and gazed out at the beauty before him. The nearly full moon had barely risen over the horizon, was quite large, and cast a good deal of light against the dark blue evening sky. He was drawn to the outside and opened the door for an even better view.

On the terrace, the night breeze brushed against his skin and the coolness was refreshing after feeling so flushed with heightened emotion. He stood out there awhile, taking in every element of the evening when he suddenly found himself walking toward the edge of the property. As he approached the green hedges, he looked over them at the seagrass where he and Lily had stood mere hours ago, full of joy and contentment in each other's company. Almost without thinking, he was propelled by some inward force to climb over the bushes and stand in that very spot, as if somehow it would restore the lost moment.

Once on the grass, he thought of nothing but Lily. She had been proud of him for this small progress. He closed his eyes and wondered how he might make things right in her eyes once again. Perhaps if he could take another step...and then other. He soon found himself standing on the threshold of the beach and a shiver crept up his spine. He had never been so far from the house on his own. One more step and he would finally feel the soft, grainy sand on his bare feet.

He raised his leg to take that final step when he heard voices in the distance on the shore. The boy and girl—Everett and Flora were the names Lily gave them—were walking on the beach and happily chattering away. He watched Everett pick up a stone and toss it in the water then begin running. He jumped effortlessly over a large piece of driftwood that had washed up on shore with the grace of a gazelle and continued without missing a beat. How carefree he seemed. Noah burned with envy at his agility and how unencumbered he was by fear or insecurity. How small his progress seemed to him now. Could he ever be that carefree and strong? He wanted to believe it was possible, but he had his doubts.

He continued watching as the two drew closer to where he was. He found the girl to be nearly as buoyant and energetic. It was no wonder Lily was drawn to them both. They were now laughing at a joke no one else could hear and didn't notice they were being watched until finally Everett looked up and saw Noah standing there and for a moment their eyes met in the darkness.

Being suddenly shaken back to reality, Noah didn't want to invite any engagement with these strangers, so he turned back to the house, quickly jumped over the hedge, and returned to the security of Birchwood Cottage. He had come so near to another breakthrough. Perhaps another day.

CHAPTER TWELVE

L ily couldn't believe how quickly things had spiraled out of control. One moment she and Noah were sharing a beautiful moment painting together on the seagrass and the next she was fleeing for home. Once she arrived, she flew through the front door of the blue cottage, past her parents, and into her bedroom. She sat on the edge of her bed, hugging her pillow close to her chest, and wept in confusion. Would she really never be invited back to Birchwood Cottage again? The thought was too much to bear.

She played the confrontation with Prissy over in her mind and still couldn't make sense of it. If nothing else, it gave her a small glimpse into Noah's predicament. Yes, he was allowing his aunt to enable his own fears, he confessed as much, but she now saw exactly what a stronghold Aunt Prissy had on the situation to begin with. Lily knew she would have to figure out a way to help her friend and that it would require patience, but for now, she was too upset to think straight. So upset, in fact, that she accidentally left her easel and paint supplies behind.

The next day she contemplated whether or not she should go back to Noah's house to retrieve her things, as it might also serve as an excuse to try and patch things up with Aunt Prissy, but something told her to hold off a bit. Instead, she decided to spend the day inside reading and catching up on chores. Her mother had fallen behind on the cleaning as she had been spending a good deal of time in town. Aside from doing the shopping, she also assisted the church ladies in putting together gift baskets for shut-ins.

"You wouldn't believe how many people in town are confined to their homes, Lily," her mother began. "It's so nice of the Reverend and his wife to want to reach out to them and bring a little joy to their circumstance. You should join me sometime. His daughter, Ruth, is such a sweet girl and about your age. You might like her for a friend."

Lily hadn't given it much thought until now but

agreed it might be a good thing to help out with. "Yes mama, I'll come with you next time if you'd like."

Her mother nodded and continued. "Interesting, I saw your friend, Noah, on the list of people they were packing baskets for. Well, he and his Aunt Priscilla…is that her name? They seem like such sad people. Their circumstance is so unfortunate."

"Yes mama, I suppose they are…" She had never thought of Noah as being a charity case, only as her friend, but in light of her recent experience it now seemed clear to her how outsiders must see them.

"A Mrs. Cartwright told me his mama died shortly after he was born, and he's been left alone with his aunt while his father takes off for work most of the year. I feel real sorry for the boy. His aunt is known as being a little bit of a crackpot. People say she never married and instead is completely devoted to that brother of hers. Apparently, she had the chance to marry once, a rather nice fellow, but her brother didn't much care for the lad, so she ran him off. Some people suspect he didn't like him because he wanted his sister for himself, to help raise poor Noah, having lost his wife and all. Isn't that just terrible?"

Lily loved her mama desperately, but like many women, she did enjoy a nice bit of gossip. Being new in town, she was probably just happy to be active and making new friends in the community, but every word she shared hurt Lily deeply. It was hard to imagine people talking about Noah in such a flippant way. Yes, the circumstance was indeed terrible, but he was so much more than a charity case and it seemed to Lily that perhaps there was a better way to help than just dropping off a gift basket once in a while.

Lily determined in her mind that she was going to be more patient and understanding with Noah, while still pushing him to be more independent. That is, if she ever had the opportunity again. Sure, he was behind her in his studies, but he had a sharp mind and was catching up quickly just in his own reading over the summer. She knew he wasn't to be underestimated, but even as is, he was sensitive and kind and cared for her a great deal. Yes, he sometimes lost his temper and reacted senselessly, but she knew it was because he had not yet learned how to properly communicate his feelings. Maybe she really could help him. He had seemed eager to try before Aunt Prissy disrupted the headway they were making.

Lily finished cleaning up the kitchen and helped her mama wash and peel some carrots for a roast, then decided to step outside for a bit and get some fresh air. The humidity of the previous week had dissipated somewhat, and the air was now crisp and pleasant. Lily walked on through the trees a short distance to find her favorite maple log to sit on. She needed a bit of time to herself to think things through about how she might proceed in the situation with Noah and his aunt. She was deep in thought when a voice startled her.

"Hey Lil, mind if I call you Lil?" It was Everett.

"Oh sure, I don't mind. My friends back home used to call me that."

Everett smiled, thinking he was quite clever. "What have you been up to? I haven't seen you in a few days. You're not mad at us are ya?" He jabbed her lightly in the arm.

Lily forced a smile. "Oh no, not in the least. I've just been dealing with some things, that's all. How have you been?"

Everett ignored the question and pressed her further, "Well, why don't you tell me about it. Maybe I can help."

Lily sighed hopelessly, "No, that's okay, this is something I probably have to figure out on my own."

"Hey, we're friends, right?" Everett prodded, giving her that lopsided grin.

Lily's tummy only did a little flip this time. "I don't know, it's just complicated…"

Everett sat down next to her. "Well, maybe together we can sort it out. Just give me an idea of what it is and I'm sure I can help. I am great at rescuing damsels in distress, you know." He added raising his arm gallantly, as though holding a sword.

Lily hesitated as he seemed to be making light of the situation, then finally gave in thinking it might actually be nice to have someone to talk to about her troubles. "Well, I have a friend named Noah. Did I tell you about Noah?" Everett shook his head (of course she hadn't). "Well, Noah is the first person I met when we moved here. He lives next door to me in the large stone cottage."

Everett's eyes lit up with recognition, "Oh yes, I believe I saw him last night. He was standing in the grass and looked a bit troubled. I was going to say hello and introduce myself, but he took off when he saw me."

Lily shook her head. "Yes, that would be him." She found it both curious and encouraging that Noah had ventured back out onto the seagrass, even after his aunt's meltdown. She considered asking more about that but then thought better of it. "You see, he is a very nice boy, but the thing is, he never wants to leave the house and have fun—like we had the other day."

"What's wrong with him? Is he lazy or something?"

"Oh no, it's more than that. I mean, he *never* leaves. His aunt cares for him and insists he is too sick to go outside but it seems to me that he isn't really sick at all, except that he doesn't get enough sunshine and exercise. Well anyway, I had been visiting him almost every day. We paint together too—he is an incredibly talented painter, just brilliant—but the other day we decided to step outside of his backyard to paint and his aunt went berserk over it and began raving like a madwoman. She blamed me for being a bad influence on him and told me to leave and that I was no longer welcome to visit. I feel awful for him because he wants to try, but she holds him back and now I don't know what to do. I only wanted to help, but I think I really got him in trouble and for all I know he'll never be able to speak to me again anyway."

Everett scratched his chin as he thought over all the things Lily said to him. If he was being honest, he felt a little pang of jealousy as she talked about Noah's talent, but decided to try and help if he could for Lily's sake. "Well, sounds to me like a real difficult situation, I'm not sure what you can do. Perhaps you can go and try to speak to his aunt about it, but it might be best to wait for the dust to settle a bit first. And if that doesn't work maybe your parents could help."

Lily didn't know how long she wanted to wait to sort things out, but perhaps Everett was on to something. "How long do you think I should wait?"

"I would suggest waiting at least a few days. Who knows, maybe it will work itself out on its own by then. Things are rarely as tragic as they seem. I bet his aunt will come around after she has time to settle down, not to mention I'm sure your friend Noah will have a talk with her as well."

Lily started going back into deep thought as she considered Everett's words. Maybe waiting would be best. Surely Aunt Prissy couldn't stay mad for long, not to mention it might be best to give Noah time to work things out himself. He knew her better than anyone and it might even do him some good to assert himself. Surely, he too believed his aunt was being unreasonable and would fight for his friendship with Lily. She had just made up her mind to follow Everett's advice when he grabbed Lily's hands and pulled her to her feet.

"It's gonna be okay Lily," Everett said offering his comfort. "Everything will work out. I'm sure you and this Noah will be painting or whatever again before you know it. In the meantime, why don't you go take a walk with me and get your mind off all this gloomy stuff? It's a beautiful day and you should enjoy it!"

Lily appreciated the show of support but wasn't quite ready to indulge in any fun. "Thank you, Everett, I appreciate it, but dinner will be ready soon enough and to be honest, I'm just not up for it right now. Perhaps another day?"

Everett looked disappointed but quickly relented as Lily seemed determined to remain focused on her concerns about Noah and he wasn't sure he wanted to continue talking about it. "Okay, I'm taking you up on that though! I'll be by soon and we'll make a day of it."

And with that, Everett was off like a shot, bounding back through the woods toward his own house before Lily could reply. She stood up and dusted off her backside and headed home as well. She wasn't even sure she could find much pleasure in anything as long as this situation with Aunt Prissy remained unresolved.

CHAPTER THIRTEEN

E verett tried to hold Lily to her word the following day, but nothing had changed. She still wasn't up for joining him on one of his expeditions. She continued wrestling with the urge to run over to Noah's house and reconcile the whole mess, but Everett said it was still too soon, reminding her that it was right to allow Noah to handle the situation with his aunt first. She figured he was right, but if she couldn't straighten things out today then she wasn't up for much else. Everett went away in defeat once again but with the promise of returning soon.

With Everett gone, Lily decided instead that it might

be nice to paint to distract herself from all her worries, but then remembered she left most of her supplies at Noah's house. The realization was disappointing, but then she thought to help her mother tend the vegetable garden the previous owners left behind. Once they pulled out the weeds and trimmed up some of the overgrowth, Lily passed the rest of the afternoon organizing the bookcase in her room. It had gotten quite out of sorts, removing and replacing books constantly, not to mention her favorite knick-knacks were already collecting dust.

The items on the shelf were an assortment of things she'd picked up over the years. Among them were her favorite seashell she found on the beach since moving to the blue cottage, a snow globe containing the Nubble Lighthouse that her father had given her three Christmases ago when they visited Maine for the holidays, a porcelain figure of a cat her friend Percy back in Virginia gave her after she commented how much it resembled a cat she once had, a silver handheld mirror that belonged to her mother as a girl, a teacup from her grandmother's china set containing a bouquet of dried wildflowers she picked near the shore, and a set of brand new drawing pencils tied with ribbon that she won in an art contest that she didn't have the heart to break in just yet.

These items conjured up many memories and

represented various seasons of her young life but also served as a reminder of how quickly time was passing. Somehow it made her sad to look at them, as though these delicate, misty memories were slipping away and things were going to change drastically. She glanced at her reflection in the handheld mirror and it was apparent that she was becoming a young lady. She pulled down her well-read copy of Peter Pan and opened it up to a passage that felt truer now than ever…

> *"All children, except one, grow up. They soon know that they will grow up, and the way Wendy knew was this. One day when she was two years old she was playing in a garden, and she plucked another flower and ran with it to her mother. I suppose she must have looked rather delightful, for Mrs. Darling put her hand to her heart and cried, 'Oh, why can't you remain like this forever!' This was all that passed between them on the subject, but henceforth Wendy knew that she must grow up. You always know after you are two. Two is the beginning of the end."*

But Lily wasn't two. She was sixteen and why had she not noticed until now that growing up was inevitable. Her feelings informed her of that. So much deeper than ever before, she had never experienced true, heartfelt sadness or love. Love? Was that what she felt for Noah? She wasn't sure, but she knew it was different somehow. She cared about Noah, truly cared for him. She didn't want to see him suffering and she didn't want to lose him. Why were tears pooling in her eyes now?

She wiped them away with the back of her hand, cursing herself for being a silly girl, and placed the book back on the shelf. Even with all her thinking and reminiscing, the answers were no clearer to her than before. Perhaps it would be good for her to get out of the house, but not today. Today she would sleep. And with that, she laid down on top of the soft quilt covering her bed and drifted off into a light slumber until she was called for dinner.

Everett returned yet again the next morning, this time he wouldn't take no for an answer. Having done her fair share of sulking over the past two days, Lily agreed to take a short walk with him through the woods but informed him that then she must get back home to prepare dessert for a late afternoon tea. Reverend Thomas's wife was stopping over to discuss some ideas with Lily's mom about the upcoming bake sale the church would be hosting to raise money to help provide clothes for some of the less fortunate children in town. Lily wanted to present her cranberry muffins as a possible contender for the sale. Mrs. Thomas would also be bringing her two daughters with her and Lily was immensely curious to meet them.

Everett agreed to have her home in time for lunch, took her by the hand, and pulled her along hastily toward the trees before she had a chance to change her mind. Even as they slowed down, Everett held Lily's hand tightly and tried to put a smile on her face by telling her a joke he overheard his father telling someone in town.

"Why is a dog like a tree?"

Lily thought about it for a minute and conceded, "Gee, I don't know! Why *is* a dog like a tree?"

"Because they both lose their bark once they're dead." Everett looked at Lily with interest, but she didn't react with laughter, rather her mouth was gaping open in shock. "What?" Everett snickered.

"That's terrible!" She exclaimed. "Just horrible!"

"Oh c'mon, it's pretty funny though, right?" he poked her in the side as if to give her a little tickle and Lily broke into light laughter. "See?"

"I guess it's *kinda* funny, but the poor dog!"

Everett hopped away from her toward a large tree. "C'mon Lil, there's something I want to show ya!"

"What is it?"

"Oh, just trust me okay?"

Lily walked over to the giant oak tree where Everett stood and watched as he quickly climbed the branches until he was quite high within its boughs. He waved her to join him and she looked up at the prospect of climbing it herself. It was a good climbing tree, but she moved a bit slower than the sprightly young boy.

Once up in the heavy branches alongside him, Everett turned her attention to the view. They were high above many of the other nearby trees and she gasped as she saw the vast blue ocean sparkling in the morning sun. "How beautiful!" She breathlessly managed to say. Indeed, it was a stunning sight, and one Everett was proud to share with his sweet friend.

He drew closer to her now, standing behind her to make sure she was secure. Lily had no fear, only awe. "I'm glad you like it," Everett remarked, his breath tickling her ear. "I came across it the other day and thought how much I would like to show it you. I haven't even shown it to Flora yet!"

Lily blushed and was so overcome with ecstasy that she almost forgot about her troubles completely for a short time. "Where is Flora anyway? I miss that sister of yours!"

"Oh, she's at home doing girl stuff...laundry."

"Girl stuff? Oh, so only *girls* can do laundry? Everett you are being just wicked today!" She would have playfully slapped him had she not thought better of the possibility that one or both of them might fall.

Everett laughed and was glad to know Lily could sense he was only teasing. He liked getting a little rise out of her, but mostly he just liked spending time with her, walking and joking around. She was smart, fun, and full of life and could give it back—so unlike many of the girls he knew before. It made him happy to know he was able to take her mind off the other boy. Besides, what good could a shut-in be for her? Lily, so wild and free-spirited, needed someone to go on adventures with and help her experience the world before her.

After a few more moments of taking in the view, Everett got beneath Lily to help guide her down from the tree. She was actually pretty good at climbing, but he felt the need to watch over her just the same.

When their feet hit the ground once again, Everett led her to the path that exited the woods and back out to the sandy beach. It was a beautiful August day, though dark clouds were looming on the horizon. The air had begun cooling considerably, but some humidity had returned with the approaching storm. They walked a ways more while Everett being his playful self, continued to tease her and look for excuses to grab her hand and so she picked up some wildflowers to keep them occupied. While she did like Everett a great deal, she was still confused about so many things.

He then provoked her further by trying to grab the flowers out of her hands as he did a few days earlier, only this time she managed to thwart his attempts and ran laughing down the beach to make her escape. Everett was not deterred by her flight and began chasing behind her. When he finally caught up to where she was, he wrapped his arms around her waist and lifted her off the ground as she squirmed in a fit of giggles. He then set her down, looking into her soft, smiling brown eyes. She tried to avert his gaze, but he kissed her lightly on the lips.

Lily was quite taken by surprise and felt immense guilt over the unexpected kiss for some reason. She stared at Everett in disbelief then shouted, "I have to go now," and ran swiftly back to her house. Everett touched his lips which were once upon Lily's and wondered if he had made a mistake.

CHAPTER FOURTEEN

The morning after their unresolved fight at dinner, Noah awoke with a slim hope that his Aunt would see things differently in the light of a new day. If she did, she wasn't communicating any such sentiment. However unlikely, he also anticipated that Lily might attempt to come see him at the usual time, despite his aunt's cruel words. Again, his hopes were dashed as noon came and went with no sign of Lily.

He stared hopelessly out at the shoreline, on the off chance he might catch a glimpse of her, when he finally decided it would be best to put his restless energy to use. He pulled out his canvas of the nearly finished painting he hoped to surprise Lily with of her standing by the shore and went to work. In doing so he noticed for the first time the paint supplies she left behind when she fled in a hurry. Noah frowned at the memory.

As he painted, his stormy mood began to affect the sunny depiction of the scene, so Noah decided to take a break and grab a bite to eat. It suddenly occurred to him that she might return after all to retrieve her belongings. Perhaps Lily would try to visit tomorrow and together they could convince his aunt once and for all that she was no real threat. Maybe his aunt would finally see what a big misunderstanding this was. And he would demonstrate it by his improving health, which Lily had already contributed to.

The following day came and went with still no sign of Lily. By day three Noah was in distress and had begun to give up hope of any reconciliation. He would have to try and speak to Aunt Prissy about it again, but even if he did convince her to go back on her threat, would Lily forgive them for the way she was treated? Noah feared he was becoming too burdensome a friend. He wouldn't blame her for never wanting to speak to him again. But then he considered the many meaningful moments they shared. Surely that couldn't mean nothing at all.

Noah knew that such thoughts would drive him crazy, as he was already exhausted from trying to work it all out. He would paint a while longer and then pack it up. His art tutor, Miss Weathervane, had been by earlier that day and was increasingly impressed with his progress. He decided to show her a couple of his latest creations, but the painting of Lily was for her eyes only—at least to begin with. He was just putting the final touches on it but didn't know how he would get the opportunity to present it to her. Still, it was the only thing pushing him forward and keeping him sane these last couple of days and he wondered what would keep his mind occupied once it was complete.

Just then, Noah heard the sound of laughter echoing off the shore. He could make out the voices of a male and female and hoped it was the brother and sister taking another stroll. But as the pair drew closer the female voice became familiar, which filled him with dread. He walked over to the hedges for a better look, shaking as he looked out. Just as he feared, it was Lily and that boy Everett, running along the sand laughing as he playfully chased her.

Noah watched in despair as Everett scooped Lily into his arms and kissed her on the lips. The blood drained from Noah's face, a cold sensation spreading throughout the inside of his trembling frame. His worst nightmare had come true and he was there to witness the whole thing. This was more than he could bear. He turned and ran into the house in a fit of rage, curses flying from his lips. He threw himself on the bed, pounding his fists on the pillow in frustration. He hated them both. He wanted to hate Lily anyway, but he definitely hated Everett.

"Why Lily, why?" he cried out in agony. His hopes for their budding relationship were now certainly dashed and it was as though there was never anything special between them. He wondered if she had only used him from the beginning—a convenient companion when there was no one else—but now with someone new to occupy her time he suddenly meant nothing to her. In fact, she probably saw this whole incident with his aunt as a fortunate opportunity to get out of the friendship. Perhaps he was better off alone after all. Maybe Aunt Prissy had been right all along. Didn't she warn him about the danger friendships could have on his health? Even now he felt dizzy and lightheaded and his throat was tightening with the strain of his emotions.

He hugged the pillow tighter and continued weeping bitter tears as the terrible scene played over and over in his mind. How had he been so stupid? Of course Lily would fall in love with that boy. *He is all the things I am not,* he thought dejectedly to himself. *I never deserved her. It's best that she's moved on and won't come around anymore because I don't think I'd ever been able to face her again after this.*

Aunt Prissy heard Noah's cries from down the hall and knocked forcibly on his bedroom door, but there was no answer. When she persisted in knocking, Noah finally called out, "Go away, I want to be alone!"

"What's going on Noah? Why are you making such a ruckus? Are you not feeling well?"

"I *said*, go away! Leave me alone!"

But Aunt Prissy continued pounding with greater force. "You open this door right now, young man! I demand you open this door!" she yelled.

A few moments passed when the door flew open violently in Aunt Prissy's face and caused her to step back in surprise. Standing before her was Noah, a crazed look in his red puffy eyes, his blonde shaggy hair a wild mess.

"What do you want?" He demanded.

Aunt Prissy regained her composure and firmly retorted, "Don't you take that tone with me, young man! What is the meaning of all this? What is going on?"

"Do you really want to know? Do you? Well, it's all your fault. *You* chased her away! *You* made her leave and never come back. All because of your crazy, irrational fears and delusions. I'll never forgive you for what you've done!"

Aunt Prissy was genuinely shocked at his sharp tone. How was it that the boy she cared and sacrificed for his entire life could talk to her in such a hateful way? She was utterly beside herself but began with a slightly softer reply. "What are you saying, Noah? Come to your senses! You know I never..."

"Just shut up!" he screamed, "I can't take it anymore. I want to be alone!" and with that, he slammed the door in his aunt's face.

She was so shaken by his spiteful show of emotion that she decided it would be best to take a step back and deal with him in the morning. She called out through the door, "That's just fine, I'm going to my room, but don't forget that it's I who have always been here for you and no one else." but Noah was no longer listening. He threw himself back on the bed, pulled the pillow over his head, and continued weeping without shame.

CHAPTER FIFTEEN

L ily ran straight to her house without stopping. What was Everett thinking? She liked Everett a great deal but did not see the kiss coming at all. Thinking back on all the flirtatious signs, she felt like an idiot for not seeing it sooner. She had been so caught up in her troubles with Noah that it didn't cross her mind that Everett had intentions of his own.

She entered the blue cottage feeling flush and breathless but continued toward her bedroom without stopping. In her haste, she didn't even notice her father sitting in his easy chair when she rushed past the living room until he called out, "Hey there pumpkin, where are you off to in such a hurry?"

She slowed her steps, but kept walking as she called out in reply, "Hi papa, I just have to go in my room and change before Mrs. Thomas and her daughters get here!"

"Well, you better be quick about it. Your mama is stressing in the kitchen and needs your help."

Lily barely caught his final words when she closed the door behind her. She really did have to dress quickly as her mother was easily overwhelmed when guests visited, but she also needed time to think. How had she gotten into such a mess of things in the short time she lived in Newland? She determined to put it from her mind until after the Thomas's left and then she would know how best to handle Everett.

After changing into a red sundress with tiny white flowers, she went out to the kitchen to pour the pre-made cranberry muffin batter into a pan and stuck it in the oven. Then she helped her mother finish setting up the table by laying down a lacy tablecloth and putting out her grandmother's pretty floral plates and saucers for tea, along with the sugar and honey. The teapot had just begun to whistle when there was a hearty knock at the door.

Mama took off her apron and led Mrs. Thomas and her daughters, Ruth and Leah, into the kitchen to have a seat.

Mrs. Thomas was in a fairly perky mood and babbling on about how busy she was that week with all her duties at the church, but Ruth and Leah sat quietly with their hands in their laps, still as mannequins. Lily noted that Ruth was quite an attractive young lady with her hair pinned up neatly on her head in the latest fashion and sporting a lovely pale blue dress with a thin black belt securing her tiny waist. Leah, on the other hand, though only a year or two younger, was dressed very plain with her hair secured in a messy braid and seemed completely preoccupied with staring at her hands.

Lily smiled at them and introduced herself in an effort to make polite conversation. Ruth returned the favor and thanked her for having them, while Leah never looked up to acknowledge Lily at all.

"Never mind Leah," Ruth said. "She is always that way. You get used to it. My mother tells me you haven't lived in Newland long. How are you liking it so far?"

Lily was relieved by Ruth's willingness to engage and replied, "I'm really enjoying it. The beaches are just stunning, and I've even made a couple of friends." She wondered if Noah would still consider her a friend if his aunt continued to forbid her to visit him.

"Oh really? I know most people in town. Have you had a chance to meet your neighbors?"

"Which ones?"

"The only ones worth discussing, as most people around here would say…Priscilla and Noah. They live in Birchwood Cottage, the big house just north of you."

"Oh yes, of course, Noah and I have become quite good friends."

"Really? So, then you know all about it?"

"If you mean about his mother dying, yes, it is very sad." Lily was suddenly uncomfortable at the thought that Noah would be the subject of gossip once again.

"Well, that and everything else. He's quite alone over there. I've known him for years and find him to be a very thoughtful and sensitive sort of boy. Why just the last time I was over he showed me some of his paintings. He's so talented, but I'm sure you must already be familiar with his giftedness." Ruth's eyes lit up as she talked about Noah's paintings.

Lily swallowed hard. She remembered Noah mentioning the Reverend's daughters, but not in any particularly glowing light. In fact, based on his description she imagined Ruth to be plain and sallow, but she was in reality quite beautiful. "Um yes, I am familiar with his work and agree, he is incredibly talented. Do you visit him often?"

"I suppose you could say that." Ruth said proudly,

"Why we were there only last week, but we plan to visit again very soon. His aunt is a bit of an eccentric, as I'm sure you know, but always kind and hospitable when we stop by."

Lily suddenly felt a bit unnerved and decided it might be a good idea to change the subject. Already her mind swirled with questions about Noah's friendship with Ruth and why he had spoken so little of her when she seemed to visit so often. Had she been mistaken in thinking she was his one and only true friend? She could certainly understand why Noah would enjoy spending time with someone as attractive and doting as Ruth. Sure, Lily was certainly aware of his good qualities, but they seemed all the more apparent hearing Ruth speak of them.

The afternoon tea went on no more than an hour when Mrs. Thomas felt she had discussed all the necessities of the upcoming bake sale. She not only loved Lily's cranberry muffins but insisted they be included in the lineup of prestigious baked goods submitted only by Newland's very best. Lily should have been more excited at the prospect, but despite her best efforts, her mind was still preoccupied with everything that transpired that day and after the Thomas's left she returned promptly to her room to mull it over. She paced anxiously as she did her best to get to the bottom of all these mixed-up feelings.

Suddenly it occurred to her that the best solution would not be found in the solitude of her bedroom but to deal with the problem head-on, face to face. Enough was enough! She was tired of waiting to hear from Noah and was going to march right over there and sort the whole thing out once and for all. She would ask about Ruth too and find out what she meant to him. She was so energized by this sudden call to action that Lily didn't even stop to put on her shoes when she took off for Birchwood Cottage. She ran barefoot through the seagrass, along the shoreline, feeling her heart pounding with every step.

Noah sulked for a good hour before getting up, his chest still aching with the realization that he certainly lost Lily for good. Never again would he allow himself to care for someone so much. Was it any wonder his father went mad with heartbreak when his mother died?

The sky was growing increasingly dark with the steady approach of storm clouds in the distance, so Noah went back out to the terrace to gather up his painting supplies. The wind was picking up, and along with churning the waves into a frenzy, his easel was rocking lightly back and forth. He was surprised it hadn't blown over by now.

When he reached for the easel, his heart ripped in two all over again as he gazed at the canvas displaying the completed artwork he'd poured himself into for the girl he loved. *The girl he loved.* He glanced up to see the spot she once stood that inspired this piece and couldn't believe his eyes. There she was at that very moment heading in his direction with great speed. He rubbed his eyes to ensure it wasn't a mere vision. What could she possibly want with him now? His mind considered many possibilities, none of them assuring.

Lily had intended to knock on the front door and confront Aunt Prissy directly but was so heartened at the sight of Noah on the terrace that she decided instead to run toward him directly so they could speak first. The elation in her spirit was quickly diffused when she saw the dark, glowering expression in Noah's countenance. "Hey," she called out to him from below. "Can we talk?"

"About what?"

Lily hadn't considered she would be unwelcomed by Noah. "About what happened the other day. We need to set things right."

"Well, if you came to collect your paint supplies you can have them right now." Though his heart swelled at the sight of Lily, Noah's emotions were heightening, and he couldn't seem to stop himself.

"Don't be silly. It's not the paint tools, Noah. It's our friendship I want to talk about!"

"Oh, do we still have a friendship? Or did you come to gloat?" His words were like bile.

Lily couldn't help but notice the glaring accusation in his eyes and didn't know why but she didn't want to waste her time on any more misunderstandings. "Gloat about what?" She replied, her hands now placed on her hips.

"You know very well! I saw you and that…that…boy…kissing. Well, if you want him you can have him because we're through!" Noah knew he was being unfair to Lily once again, but he couldn't contain his hurt at the memory of her encounter with Everett.

Lily was shocked to learn Noah had seen her and Everett earlier that day and opened her mouth to explain but before she could form a single syllable Noah became wild and erratic.

"Don't deny it, Lily. Admit I was right! You have found someone better to spend your time with and it's clear you never really cared for me at all. Now take your things and go." Noah then heaved her paint supplies over the hedge in dramatic fashion.

Lily was shocked and wanted to react in kind but knew it wouldn't help the circumstance. "Noah," she said calmly, "knock it off this instant and listen to me. I have thought of nothing else these past few days except how to repair this situation with your aunt. Everett is a friend…"

The very mention of Everett's name sent Noah into a state of hysteria, "Oh I suppose you were thinking only of me when you threw yourself at that boy the first chance you got?" he screamed, "Do you know what I've been doing every day since you left? I was finishing this…" he turned the painting around to show her, "It's a portrait of *you*. It was a day I wanted us both to remember forever so I've been working on it for weeks as a gift. A gift for someone I thought was my friend. Someone I thought cared about me as well. Well, you know what? It's trash now! Nothing but trash!" his voice cracked.

The painting was truly a masterpiece, without question Noah's best piece yet, and Lily was amazed by its astounding beauty. She was touched that such an incredible painting was done in her honor and tears filled her eyes as she gazed upon it, but they were soon replaced by a look of horror. Before she had a chance to express her love of it, Noah took a large brush, dipped it carelessly in red paint, and splattered a large X over his precious work of art. Lily gasped in stunned disbelief at all that was transpiring and the ease with which he ravaged this gift. Noah had become a heartless monster in her view and no longer deserving of an explanation.

"How could you?" She screamed. "Your jealous ways have caused enough problems and misunderstandings between us, and this time you've gone too far Noah Sullivan! I have nothing left to say to you except goodbye forever!" And with that, Lily quickly gathered her paint supplies and turned to run back home, convinced she would never step foot in Birchwood Cottage as long as she lived.

Noah immediately regretted his actions but stood paralyzed by the deep look of hurt in Lily's eyes. How could he cause the girl he loved so much pain? His behavior was unforgivable, even to himself.

CHAPTER SIXTEEN

Once Lily reached her own home again, she was startled to find Everett standing outside the doorway waiting for her. She was so emotionally distraught that the very sight of him sent furious tears streaming down her rosy little cheeks.

"What's wrong Lily?" Everett asked, surprised by this reaction in her. "I wanted to come by and talk to you after what happened today."

"Oh Everett, it was too awful for words! My friendship with Noah, it's over! It's over for good!"

Everett approached Lily and wrapped his strong arms

around her to offer his comfort. In her distressed state, she welcomed the gesture and fell into his embrace, sobbing as she recalled the events that had transpired only moments ago. Everett had never seen such a heart-wrenching display. He didn't speak, but listened intently, not understanding every word, but one thing was becoming increasingly clear; Lily loved Noah, not him.

Noah couldn't believe the way he had behaved and placed his head in hands, shaking it in defeat. Just as he was about to succumb to utter devastation at losing Lily for good, he heard a blood-curdling scream come from inside the house. It was Aunt Prissy. He rose quickly and ran to the source of the noise immediately. When he entered the foyer, he saw a man in uniform standing in the doorway and Aunt Prissy on her knees staring at a letter in disbelief. A cold chill ran down Noah's spine and for a moment he was too terrified to speak for fear of what news this man brought.

"What is it?" he finally asked with trembling in his

voice.

Before the officer could answer his aunt cried out in a fit of anguish, "It's your father! My brother. My poor, poor brother. He is lost at sea and assumed dead." Aunt Prissy then began to wail, the sound of her cries echoing loudly throughout the hall.

Noah couldn't move or think. First this horrific incident with Lily and now his father. It couldn't be true. His father was going to be home soon and the two of them were going to finally talk things out and it would be the start of a new relationship. He had so little time with him. There was still so much to say.

Noah appeared stoic and calm, but inside he was anything but. His aunt's hysterical reaction was enough emotional display for both of them and after a few polite words exchanged with the officer, Noah sent him on his way and closed the door. After getting his aunt to calm down enough to get back on her feet, Noah led her carefully to the bedroom and helped her lie down.

"Oh Noah," she cried. "Whatever shall we do?"

Noah didn't answer because he was still in shock at the news and could not yet discuss it. The pain was coming on too strong, and in his desperation, he could think of nothing but running to Lily for the support his aunt could not offer him.

What a fool he had been, what a jealous, childish fool! Suddenly everything seemed so unimportant. Noah's world was shattering, and he needed his friend beside him more than ever. Maybe it wasn't too late to make things right, but it would take every bit of strength Noah had to muster to do what he needed to do next.

Strangely and silently, he turned away from his aunt and coolly replied, "I have to go..." and left the room with a determined step. Aunt Prissy screamed after Noah to come back and stay with her, but he was already gone. Gone down the hall, gone into the foyer, gone through the entryway, and gone out the door.

He entered the early evening air and headed into the trees, toward the blue cottage and off to see Lily. She was his only source of joy in this wretched world. He began to run now, his love for her pushing him on as never before as everything around him became a blur. His only focus was getting to Lily. He was ready now to prove how much she meant to him—how much he needed her. But when he broke through the trees, he came upon a scene his mind truly was not ready to handle on top of everything else—Lily was so soon back in Everett's arms in a tight embrace. He was too late after all.

Lily looked up in utter disbelief at the sight of Noah

standing before her house, staring back at the pair. Before she could speak, he took off again into the trees. He had to get away immediately. Lily tried to chase after him, but Everett held her back before she could budge. Instead, she called out his name over and over. "Noah! Noah!" Noah was sure he only imagined it, though her voice rang loudly in his ears.

He ran and ran as never before, but not in the direction of Birchwood Cottage. He was like a wild animal who had been caged up and finally set free. Something primitive arose inside and he headed out toward the sea. The storm was coming on fast and furious now. The clouds were dark and looming and the waves had grown to nearly ten feet, but Noah took little notice. He had read somewhere that there is nothing more dangerous than a man with nothing to lose, but Noah wasn't yet a man and barely more than a boy in his mind. None of that mattered any longer though. He was tired of being weak. Tired of being trapped in fear and hopelessness. If he was going to die, then so be it!

With that thought at the helm of his mind, Noah removed his shoes and stepped onto the cool sand. He walked with purpose, with each step savoring the new sensation of soft grains between his toes. He now understood why it held such great appeal for people, but he couldn't stop to enjoy the experience. He pressed on and came to the shoreline itself and the sand began to transform from soft and dry to firm and wet. He shuddered at the sound of each wave as it crashed powerfully before him. He had never been so near to them, but this was his moment. Sink or swim, he was not going to be a bystander in his own life any longer. He was going to live, even if only for a day!

And without another moment's hesitation, he dove mindlessly into the rushing, dangerous sea. For a moment he reveled in the pleasure of feeling the cool ocean water on his skin at last, and the taste of salt on his tongue as the spray hit his face. The boy who was once paralyzed by fear now knew no fear at all. Something inside propelled him forward as he began wading further out, embracing each surge that came over him. He felt in total control, but it wasn't long before he was overwhelmed by the depth and began to struggle against the waves, for he did not know how to swim. The waves began sucking him out further with each roll and Noah couldn't fight his way back. It soon looked like today he might sink.

After Lily broke free from Everett's grip, she began to run toward the trees where Noah exited, but just before she reached them, she saw Aunt Prissy running to her frantically. "Is Noah here?" she cried out in desperation.

"No, I thought he headed for home!" Lily replied, concern rising up inside her.

"I didn't see him on my way over here. Did he say anything to you?" Aunt Prissy seemed raving mad.

Lily shook her head, "He left before I had a chance to talk to him. What's going on?"

Aunt Prissy handed Lily the piece of paper and she read it quickly. As she digested the contents of the letter, she understood everything. He had come to tell her that his father was missing at sea and instead found her in the arms of another. *How devastated he must be*, she thought. Her anger toward Noah dissipated in light of the current tragedy with his father and she could think of nothing but going to him.

"Do you have any idea where he might have gone?" Everett interjected.

Lily thought for a moment when suddenly a look of dread filled her eyes. "Oh no," she said softly under her breath, "I'm gonna go get papa!"

"Papa!" Lily screamed as she entered the house filled with fear. Her dad rose up from the easy chair he was lounging in with a start.

"What is it pumpkin, what's going on?"

"I need you to come right away papa, I think Noah is in trouble!"

Lily's Dad quickly slipped his shoes on and flew out the door in the direction where Lily was headed. For her, he couldn't move fast enough. She waved Everett and Aunt Prissy to follow her as well, all four of them running to the shore to beat the devil. She had a feeling deep in her gut that Noah was in grave danger and there was no time to lose.

CHAPTER SEVENTEEN

N oah fought hard to keep his head above the waves, but the sand he stood upon was getting sucked out from beneath him and he began to lose his footing with each churn of the choppy sea. The weight of his wet clothes made it all the more difficult to stay afloat. To and fro he was tossed about as the waves consumed him, over his head and swallowing him up just to spit him back out again. Noah continued fighting but was beginning to lose both the strength and the will for survival when suddenly he heard a muffle of voices in the distance. Noah tried shouting back for help, but it was futile, he could no longer get his head above water long enough to do so and was going under for good.

For a moment there was nothing but darkness. Noah accepted his fate and cursed himself for what a fool he was from the beginning of his life to the end. Now the struggle would soon be over, and he would join his mother and father in a better place. Maybe he and his father would have that talk after all. Noah may not have given God much thought in his life, but he always believed in Him. He was told his mother and father met in church, so he figured they must be in heaven, and that's where he wanted to go.

Noah's entire life began to rapidly flash before his eyes when suddenly he saw a bright light. But it wasn't at the end of a tunnel to some celestial palace in the sky, it was the late afternoon sun blinding his vision. There was a break in the clouds which allowed the sunlight to shine directly on Noah's face. He couldn't recall how he ended up there, but Noah realized he was laying on the wet sand and could hear voices from every direction. Feeble and faint, he searched for Lily. There she was, holding his hand, tears streaming down her angelic face.

"Don't move Noah, just relax," she said. "Everything is going to be alright—I promise."

He only had enough strength to reply with, "I'm sorry Lily, I'm so sorry." before the blackness returned.

When Noah awoke, he was laying in his own bed. His head hurt terribly, and he had no concept of time, but at least he recognized his surroundings. It was silent with no other sound than the hum of dead air. He tried sitting up but was physically too weak and quickly became light-headed. He laid his head back down on the soft pillow. He couldn't quite figure how long he'd been out, but gauging from the fresh pair of clean, striped pajamas he was wearing, Noah figured it couldn't have been long.

Just about the time he began wondering when he could speak to someone who had answers, the door to his room opened and Dr. Fitzgerald entered, his physician for as long as he could remember.

"Well, well, well, you're awake I see…that's wonderful news!"

"How long have I been out, doctor?" Noah sounded hoarse when he spoke.

"It's been about 48 hours. You're a very lucky boy, you

know."

Noah could remember very little about the events from a couple of days ago, but they slowly started coming back to him as he recalled the letter his aunt received. "Will I be okay?" He asked.

The doctor responded, "Well, there are still some reasons to be concerned. You almost drowned you know. If that boy Everett hadn't gotten to you on time, you'd be a goner for sure. We managed to get the water out of your lungs, but we're still concerned your immune system was so weakened by all the trauma you've endured that you might be coming down with a case of bronchitis. You've been through a great deal and your body is having a difficult time fighting like it should, so it's imperative that you take it easy."

Noah was unsure what to make of everything the doctor said and was still trying to process all that occurred, especially the part where Everett saved his life. It was a hard pill to swallow but he now knew he had Everett to thank for still being alive. That most certainly made him a hero in Lily's eyes, and well deserved too. He then wondered how Aunt Prissy was taking all this.

The doctor then spoke and answered at least one of his inner-questions. "As it turns out your aunt is in no state to care for you at this time, having suffered her own trauma. She too is resting in her room for now. The Reverend's daughter, Ruth Thomas, has offered to help out during your recovery. Apparently, she knows you and your aunt well. She'll be in a bit later with a little something to eat, but like I said, just take it easy."

A few minutes later Ruth entered with a tray containing a bowl of hot soup and a tall glass of water. Noah suddenly realized how raw his throat was and reached out for a drink. Ruth could see it was the water he was grasping for and Noah thanked her as he took the glass from her tiny hands and proceeded to guzzle it down.

After he set it down, Ruth sat beside Noah on a chair next to the bed and asked how he was feeling.

"Not so great, to be honest. My head is killing me."

"I'm sorry to hear it," was her sympathetic reply. "I assume the doctor told you what a close call it was."

"Yes, he did. I feel so stupid, to be honest."

"Stupid? Why? It could honestly happen to anyone. Many people succumb to waves of that size."

"No, it's not the waves," Noah sighed, "It's the reason I did it. I guess I felt like I had something to prove." He looked up and saw the caring expression in Ruth's green eyes and felt she posed no threat to his ego. "I guess I was just sick of feeling like I wasn't living. I wanted to know what it was like to swim in the ocean like everyone else. I suppose I could have picked a better time to try, huh?"

Ruth smiled warmly at him and reassured him that he could try again when he was better and that she was actually proud of him for being brave. Noah didn't feel brave but had little energy left to protest and decided he should spend it on trying to eat a little.

"It's important you get your strength back up," Ruth said, as she helped sit him up. "You can just leave the tray on the nightstand when you're through and I'll pick it up later. She hesitated a moment before asking, "Would you like me to come back after you've rested and keep you company for a bit?"

"That would be nice," Noah said, though it was Lily he really wished to see. He didn't feel ready to ask about Lily just yet though. He was still exhausted, and it wasn't long after he ate some of the soup that he was fast asleep once again; dreaming of the great ocean waves beckoning him to return to the sea, but the voice calling his name was Lily's.

Lily had been going mad for two days with worry. Ever since the incident where Noah almost drowned, she had struggled to forgive herself for everything that transpired and her own lack of compassion for his situation. She demanded too much from this young man who had known so little of the world. She should have been more patient and understanding, but maybe it was too late.

Once she got word from Dr. Fitzgerald that Noah would pull through, he just needed his rest before receiving visitors, she was able to breathe a sigh of relief and consider how she might make it up to him. The last thing she wanted to remember was the hurt look in his eyes and she wondered how she might be a comfort to him in his time of need, especially now that she heard about Aunt Prissy's frazzled mental state and her inability to care for him properly. She was glad to know that Reverend Thomas's daughter, Ruth, would be a help to them both, even though it hadn't totally escaped her attention that she was a beautiful caregiver. She couldn't worry about that now though. Noah's health is what mattered most, and she had to go see Everett so they could talk.

She walked over to his house and knocked on his door, but his mother answered and informed her that he and Flora had gone out for a walk a bit ago. Lily decided to see if she could find them and proceeded to head toward the trails in the woods they had visited only a couple of days ago when Everett kissed her.

She went past the tree they climbed together, and Everett and Flora were nowhere to be seen. The woods were still and unsettling, despite being midday. No presence of young people seemed to inhabit them, so she headed back for the shore. Just beyond the opening of the woods, under a rock formation, she saw Everett and Flora romping along the sand, splashing their feet in the surf and laughing as they sprayed each other with the salty mist.

"Everett, Flora!" Lily called out, waving her hand. They looked up and saw her and waved back so she continued onward to join them.

"Hey Lil," Everett called out as she approached, still in a jovial mood despite the stormy look on her face. Flora seemed delighted to see Lily as well, oblivious as usual.

"Hey, you two, I'm glad I found you, I need to talk to Everett."

"Oh really?" Everett spoke in a silly British accent. "Come to join us in a bit of revelry? My sister and I would love to amuse you with a dance recital." He then picked up a pile of dry seaweed on the shore, placing it on his head like hair, and pranced around like a ninny to Flora's utter delight.

"I'm serious Everett, please." Lily was not in the mood

for Everett's childish antics.

Everett took the seaweed off his head but did little to assure Lily that he was willing to take her seriously, "Goodness milady," he continued in the British accent. "Don't you look positively grim!"

Flora continued to giggle adding in a not-nearly-as-perfected accent, "Yes, what on earth do we owe the pleasure of your acquaintance? Would you like to join us in a song?" She then proceeded to sing out in an exaggerated high-pitched soprano which Everett found amusing. He liked that his sister always played along with him.

Lily shook her head. "No, I need to talk to Everett please…alone."

Everett nodded to Flora, indicating she should leave. Flora gave a pouty look but left just the same. "Tell Ma I'll be back at the house in a bit." He called after her, to which she stuck her tongue out at him playfully.

"So, what is it?" Everett finally said once the two of them were alone.

"It's about the other day…" Lily began.

"Oh, the kiss?" He replied boldly.

Lily blushed. "Yes, we'll get to that, but first I wanted to thank you for saving Noah's life. I didn't get a chance to properly convey my gratitude. I know you've never met him, but he means a great deal to me."

"I sorta got that impression by now," Everett said flatly.

Lily got Everett to continue walking along the shore as they talked. "Yes, well, you mean a great deal to me as well. I can never thank you enough for what you did."

Everett shrugged his shoulders. "It's nothing. I saw someone in trouble so I did what I could. Is that all? I really need to get home soon." It was clear Everett was uncomfortable with the seriousness of the conversation.

"Yes, you can go in a minute, but about the other thing…" Lily kicked the sand at the mention of the kiss.

"That was nothing too, don't sweat it, Lily. You're a great girl and I like you, but I thought we were just having fun. So, everything's okay?"

In some ways, Lily didn't know what she expected Everett to say about it but was surprised by his aloofness. Perhaps she overestimated his feelings after all. Deep down she was relieved though and nodded emphatically. "Yes, everything is fine. I am glad we can still be friends."

"Of course, we can Lil," Everett turned his eyes from facing Lily and was surprised by the pain in his chest at the confirmation that Lily only wanted to be friends. He had never cared about such things before. "Well, I guess I better run, but let's hang out soon!" he called out as he trotted away for home, leaving Lily thankful for the way the discussion went.

She too decided to head for home, her thoughts now turned to Noah. She contemplated all the things she would say to him when he was well enough to have visitors, as well as all the things they might do together now that he had finally set himself free from the confines of Birchwood Cottage. She prayed silently that the drowning incident wouldn't cause him to go backward in his progress, but something told her that the taste of freedom would be too great to be overshadowed by that unfortunate turn of events.

She entered the door of the blue cottage when she saw her mother and father in a serious discussion. "Hello mama and papa," she called out, but they just looked at her. "What is it?" She asked, sensing something serious was afoot.

Her father looked anxious, "We're so glad you're home, honey. Please sit down, your mama and I have something to tell you."

CHAPTER EIGHTEEN

Noah awoke several hours later feeling quite fevered. His face was burning up, dampening his pillow with perspiration. The blankets were a mess from all his tossing and turning. Ruth heard him stirring and came quickly to his bedside, a fresh glass of water in hand.

"Is everything okay, Noah, can I get you anything?"

"Just water please," he replied weakly and thanked her as she handed him the cool glass.

"You're not looking too good. Should I get the doctor?"

Noah wasn't sure and decided to wait a few minutes

before giving her an answer. He laid there silently, trying to regain his wits, and watched as Ruth tenderly placed the covers back over him properly. "Has anyone else been by to visit?"

"Yes, everyone has been very concerned with your wellbeing Noah, but the doctor said it's probably best not to receive visitors until you've had a chance to recover a bit."

"What about…"

"Lily? Yes, she is very anxious to see you. She's been by three times already." Ruth had been made quite aware of Noah's significance to Lily the past couple days.

Noah felt a bit of comfort in knowing that she had made so many attempts to visit and hadn't missed the opportunity to see him of her own accord. "I still don't know exactly what happened," Noah lamented.

"Well, the story has been told several times to the doctors and authorities, so I could tell you what I overheard if you'd like."

"Yes please." Noah felt content hearing it from Ruth rather than someone directly involved. The idea of hearing it from Lily or his aunt made him cringe with embarrassment.

Noah braced himself as Ruth explained the whole situation as it went down on everyone else's end. She talked about how Aunt Prissy came looking for him at Lily's house after he fled, how Lily was very upset by the news of his father gone missing, that it was Lily who figured out where he went, and how she ran to get her father and the four of them went to look for Noah on the beach.

"When they got there, you were struggling terribly in the water. Your Aunty Prissy was quite hysterical, as was Lily. Her father intended to go in after you, but her friend Everett wasted no time and beat him to the water. He jumped into the surf and swam quickly toward you before Mr. Stephens had the chance, good thing he did too. He said by the time he reached the spot you were at you were no longer visible. It was quite dark in the water and he couldn't see anything due to the large waves and dark sky, so he dove under and swam around blindly until he found you. Everett pulled you up out of the water, dragged you to the shore and Mr. Stephens turned you on your side and slapped you on the back until you coughed up some water. You hadn't been under long, so you quickly regained consciousness, but it was definitely a miracle that you survived!"

Noah didn't recall a single moment of the story Ruth shared, except opening his eyes to the light of the sun, but it explained why his back was sore. He felt foolish and ashamed and assumed everyone would now think even less of him for causing such a ruckus with his thoughtless behavior. Certainly, Lily could never respect him now. Everett was the real hero and deserved her love and admiration. He deserved Noah's too, for he would not still be here if it had not been for Everett's bravery. It was time to grow up.

Ruth let Noah rest a little longer while she prepared a light dinner for him and his aunt, but Noah had very little appetite and didn't eat much. The doctor came in a bit later and checked his temperature. He did indeed have a fever and was urged to get some sleep while his body fought off any possible infection. It didn't take much to convince Noah to rest as he was already drifting off.

By the next morning, the fever broke and Noah's appetite had returned, so he was eager to take down the flavorless oatmeal that Ruth prepared for him. They sat and chatted a bit. Ruth was actually quite friendly and pleasant, though they didn't speak about anything particular. He found that they might be good friends after all. He was reminded once again how wrong he had been about her all these years.

Their conversation eventually turned to Noah's

favorite topic—art. It was Tuesday and Noah was lamenting that he had to miss out on his painting lessons with Miss Weathervane. He was just saying how much he was looking forward to picking up a brush again after his recovery when Ruth interrupted him. "I have a surprise for you. Wait right here!"

Noah chuckled. "Where would I go?" That was the first time he had smiled since the whole ordeal.

Ruth rushed back into the room holding a canvas, the back of it facing Noah so he couldn't see what she was carrying.

"What is it?"

"You'll see. I saved it from the rain." Ruth flipped the canvas around and Noah saw it was the painting he had done of Lily, now marked with the red-painted X over it. "It was quite wet, but I brought it in, wiped it down, and put it by the fire to dry off. I know it seems you were not happy with it, but I wanted to tell you what a stunning painting it seems to be. Yes, it would be very lovely indeed...I really think you should fix it if at all possible." Because of the markings, Ruth didn't recognize Lily as the girl in the painting, only recognized the beauty in Noah's skill, and wanted to encourage him in his current state.

Noah once again regretted what he'd done to damage

the artwork and appreciated Ruth's efforts to save it. "We'll see, thank you." He said nothing more about it. Ruth set the painting against the wall near his bed and proceeded to sit down.

As much as Noah was enjoying Ruth's company, he was feeling fatigued once again and was just about to tell her he needed to rest a bit when there was a knock at the door. Ruth got back up to answer it and on the other side was Lily, peering over her shoulder to finally catch a glimpse of her ailing friend. Noah sat up straight in his bed and stared at her in disbelief. He had not prepared mentally for her visit, so he wanted to collect his thoughts a bit. He tried to quickly run his hands through his shaggy hair to seem at least a bit presentable, but it did little to improve his appearance.

Lily nodded gratefully to Ruth as she left the room so the two of them could talk in privacy. Noah couldn't help but notice how terrible Lily looked as well. Her hair was unbrushed and her eyes were red. He had never seen her looking so pitiful.

"Hello Noah," she said, trying to keep her composure. "how are you feeling?"

"Fine, considering. Well, it's been rough, but I suppose it's what I deserve."

"That's not true," Lily said, reaching out to place her

hand on top of his.

He looked pained. "Lily, you have no idea how sorry I am for what I've put you through. I don't even deserve…"

"Please Noah, don't say it. I know there have been a lot of misunderstandings and if only I had made you listen then perhaps this wouldn't have happened."

"Don't take the blame on yourself. You did nothing except try to help and encourage me and I treated you terribly. You have the right to be friends, or whatever, with whomever you choose. I take full responsibility for my behavior."

"Noah, listen." Lily was silent for a moment. "Whatever you think you saw. Well, it wasn't what you think. Everett and I truly are just friends."

Noah had difficulty believing this in light of what his own eyes witnessed. "Yeah, but…"

"But nothing. Everett is a fine person, but I'm too young to be seriously involved with anyone. Besides, I have some news. Oh, Noah, this is terribly hard."

Noah's chest tightened before he even had a chance to hear what it was. The look on Lily's face told him everything. "What is it?"

"My father. He's been offered a position in Boston and it starts right away. He just found out this morning."

This was the final blow in a series of devastating

disappointments. "When are you leaving?" He managed to choke out.

"In a few days. We just have to finish packing. Noah, it's so unfair! With everything we've been through, and now with the news of your father. I wish more than anything I could be here for you through it all." Tears welled up in Lily's doleful eyes.

Noah didn't know what to say. He had wasted his time being concerned about petty things when he should have been enjoying every moment they had together. Now that opportunity was lost and fate was dragging Lily far from his presence. "Will I ever see you again?"

"Yes, the good news is we are keeping the house and father says we may come back in the summer. There is also a chance we may visit in the spring and if we do, I'll be sure to come see you first thing." It was a glimmer of hope anyway, no matter how small.

Noah took Lily's hand and squeezed it tightly. "Lily, I have to tell you this now in case I don't get another chance. I know I've messed up badly, and I know I've been weak, but I am going to do everything I can to make it up to you. I am going to be a better person so that you are proud to call me your friend again. I want to be worthy of that honor."

"You always have been," came Lily's soft reply.

CHAPTER NINETEEN

Just like that, Lily was gone. Perhaps for good. Noah spent the next couple of days resting so that he would be well enough to see her off. On the day of the Stephens family's departure, there was a small going away party which included Everett, Flora and their parents, Reverend Thomas and his wife, plus their daughter's Ruth and Leah, and of course, Noah and Aunt Prissy.

Aunt Prissy had done her best to apologize to Lily for all the hurt she caused. She was still not well and prone to fits of emotional outbursts but was making an effort. She and Noah had a long talk one afternoon after lunch. She was a broken shell since the news of her brother. Reverend Thomas said of Aunt Prissy's state that she must feel a lot like Job when he said, "What I feared most has come upon me." Noah didn't know much about Job, but it sounded about right.

Dr. Fitzgerald had been tending to Prissy since the night of the incident as she was quite hysterical and inconsolable for hours on end. He strongly suggested she get some rest and follow it up with some medical assistance for her mental and emotional wellbeing. Aunt Prissy agreed to see the doctor he recommended, but only because she wanted to help Noah in whatever way she could. Despite all the years of keeping him isolated from the world, he believed she truly did love him in her own way and now his aunt was all he had. But even the stability of their situation was dubious at best. He knew things might be better if she truly got the help she needed, but only time would tell.

In the meantime, Noah needed to concentrate on his own mental and physical wellbeing. His first priority was getting out of bed and going over to Lily's house, which was still a real challenge as he was no longer riding on the adrenaline that propelled him over there the evening of the incident. But there was another factor that concerned him; facing Everett for the first time since he saved his life. That would be difficult in its own way, but selfishly he also did not want to share his final moments with Lily with anyone else. Under the circumstance, he really had no choice though.

With Aunt Prissy's help, Noah was able to keep his composure as he headed through the trees and over to the blue cottage. He credited his aunt with trying to be strong for his sake and not make a fuss. She knew this a difficult moment for Noah and was sympathetic enough to keep her worries to herself. She had spoken less in the last several days than she had in years, an effect of the shock she endured.

When Noah arrived, Lily approached him with much enthusiasm. She was wearing a navy-blue dress fashioned after a sailor's suit, with white stripes on the collar and the hem. Her soft brown curls were pulled neatly back into a bouncy ponytail, and aside from the tears glistening in her eyes, she was quite pink from the joy of seeing Noah make such strides for her sake. She threw her arms around his neck gently and thanked him for coming.

"I'd go anywhere for you!" Noah said, trying to remain upbeat. Lily returned the kind sentiment with a tender kiss on the cheek that made Noah blush.

Aunt Prissy also embraced Lily and then joined the rest of the group waiting by the house. This gave Lily and Noah a couple of minutes alone, which he was grateful for.

"It's gonna be hard, ya know," Lily began. "Not seeing

you practically every day, not seeing *this*..." She motioned to the shore.

Noah took her hands in his. "Yes, I am certain things will never be the same around here, but I don't regret a moment of it, Lily. You came in like a burst of sunshine in my life and it's like I didn't even know I was in darkness. You changed how I see myself, how I see the world, and you make me want to be a better person...to be a better man. I'll always be grateful for that."

Lily couldn't stop the tears now. It seemed like she was crying a lot these days. So many emotions for one so young, but she was deeply touched by Noah's words and expressed her own appreciation for his friendship and encouragement. He made her feel seen and accepted, a rare gift in itself, and she didn't take it for granted. They once again exchanged sentiments of grief over their pending separation, along with promises to keep in touch, then walked hand in hand to join the others. Noah could face Everett now.

When the two of them reached the group, Noah immediately approached Everett and held out a hand to shake his. Everett returned the gesture and gripped his hand tightly as Noah said, "Thank you Everett, I know we haven't had a chance to meet properly yet, but I have to thank you for saving my life. Lily has told me so many nice things about you and I hope we can be friends."

Everett gave Noah his signature lopsided grin and pulled him in for a hug. "Absolutely my friend. I'm just glad you're okay! Let's not go swimming in any storms together for a while though."

Noah laughed at this in agreement and all his fears and trepidations about Everett dissipated. He had been wrong once again in his judgments and was resolved to not be so hasty in his assessments of people in the future.

Flora came bounding alongside Everett, her raven black tight curls bouncing on her shoulder as she moved, and also introduced herself, "Hi, I'm Flora, Everett's sister. I'm the smart one."

"Ha-Ha!" Everett scoffed while punching his little sister playfully on the arm. "I bet that smarts!"

Flora stuck her tongue out at him and retorted in jest. "He's such a dope. Anyway, how did it feel to almost die?"

Everyone was silent at the brazen nature of the question, unsure of how Noah would respond, but he just chuckled, "Well, I honestly don't remember much, but it's true what they say about your life flashing before your eyes. I had a lot of weird thoughts and then everything went black."

"Wow sounds kinda spooky. Glad you made it!"

Noah liked this funny, outspoken cherub-faced girl.

He could see why Lily was so quick to call them friends. Now perhaps he would be able to do the same.

They stood around chatting for about forty minutes, awaiting the inevitable, when Lily's father made it clear it was time to go. There was a final round of hugs, some tears. Lily approached Noah to say her farewell, but before she could speak, he said, "Never say goodbye because goodbye means going away and going away means forgetting."

She knew the reference of the quote immediately and gave him one final hug. As the family sped away toward new horizons, Noah and Lily's eyes met for the last time, she waved sadly to him and she was out of his life.

CHAPTER TWENTY

With Lily gone, Noah was keenly aware of the emptiness she left behind. He descended into a deep state of melancholy, which he mostly coped with by picking up a brush. To occupy the time, he decided to take Ruth's advice to repair the painting he had so thoughtlessly ruined. It only made him miss Lily more. Still, he found a strange comfort in keeping her image before him. He could almost pretend she wasn't nearly three hundred miles away.

Noah was getting out of the house more and taking walks around the vicinity, exploring his hometown for the first time in his life. It saddened his heart that he couldn't share this experience with Lily. He would often wander over to the empty blue cottage, longing to see her emerge and join him, but instead settled on imagining what her daily life there was like since he never had the chance to see for himself. As he walked around the cozy little cottage, he contemplated which window might have led to her bedroom but wouldn't peer in for he felt it would be an invasion of privacy, even if the Stephens's no longer occupied the home. No, he preferred to wait and see the inside when he was invited over properly by Lily and her family.

But visiting the blue cottage so often only fed Noah's melancholy further. The realization that the summer season was coming to an end and his father would not be coming home contributed to his low spirits. There had been no further news of his father's whereabouts and both he and Aunt Prissy were losing hope that he survived the wreck. Sometimes he imagined what their conversations might be if he ever did get a chance to see him again, but it seemed useless to imagine and eventually he tried to put it from his mind.

The air had become increasingly cooler and the days of swimming in the sea were behind the people of Newland. Everyone was preparing for the winter months ahead, while Noah was focused on his studies. Along with furthering his painting skills, he was actually looking forward to hitting the books to work at improving his grades. He only had another year before graduation and didn't want to waste the opportunity. He would be turning a year older in a month. Time was marching on with or without him, but now he vowed to not be left behind.

In the meantime, he intended to spend the final days of summer enjoying the quiet solitude of nature. He was still easing into this new way of living and didn't want to worry his aunt too much, so he tried to stick close to home for the most part. Noah embraced the security of knowing this was one way he could expand his territory without having to face people, but Lily haunted those woods. Her presence lingered wherever she once stood. He recalled the many adventures Lily told him about and even managed to discover some of the places she had described all on his own. How much Noah wanted to shout his excitement to her in those moments, but instead was forced to save it for future letters.

Aunt Prissy was doing much better since she started seeing the doctor that was recommended. She seemed to finally be working through some of her phobias, anxieties, and grief, but she still had her moments of instability. Noah didn't want to push her too hard while she was still so fragile, so he usually let her say her piece, and eventually, she would apologize for being a "foolish old woman"—as she often referred to herself. He had really stepped up as the man of the house, reversing roles as his aunt's caregiver but she didn't seem to mind. She was tired of fighting Noah's thirst for freedom and now that her dear brother was feared dead, she found some relief in being released from the promise she made to him so many years ago.

Noah was still in recovery himself and struggled to be totally self-sufficient, so Ruth was there to help him with some of the cooking and house cleaning as well. As his health improved, he picked up the chores where he could, and they often worked together. He was both grateful for her help and enjoyed her company. In time they became good friends.

He learned so much about Ruth and her upbringing. Her parents were fine, respectable folks that were very invested in the ministries at church and expected their daughters to be as well. It's not that they didn't let them indulge in any earthly pleasures, such as pretty clothes, books, and sweets, or allow them free time to indulge in their "little hobbies", but duty was of great importance to the Thomas's and sometimes Ruth felt she didn't get to choose much for herself. She wasn't even certain what she'd want to do if given the option.

Ruth spoke often of God and loved helping people out in the community, but it seemed like there might be more—

something just for her. The more she and Noah spent time together the more he encouraged her to figure out what she was good at. It was through his nudging that she realized her passion for sewing. She had recently started making her own clothes and loved it. Her mother had shown her how to operate a sewing machine when she was ten years old with the purpose of having her assist in making blankets for missionaries, but in time she also enjoyed making clothes for her sister's dolls and pleated skirts to complement her ever-growing, fashionable wardrobe. She even designed several costumes to be used in the annual Christmas nativity at church and was proud of how they were turning out.

After speaking to Noah about the joy it brought her, Ruth decided, based on his nudging, to ask her mother if there might be a way to utilize her hobby to help the church in a more personal way. Noah found it inspiring to watch Ruth grow as a person and it felt good to be a part of that process. It was a journey they were on together in some ways.

They spent many afternoons talking and she did her best to support him with his art and studies, though she didn't quite have the interest in those things as Lily did. Ruth wasn't particularly witty, but she was always pleasant and doted on Noah endlessly. It felt good to be with someone who enjoyed his company and seemed to admire him so much. Ruth admitted she always found his shyness quite cute and secretly hoped they might be friends one day, which caused him to blush deeply.

The Reverend and his wife were over now twice a week to check on poor Aunt Prissy, and she too conceded she had been wrong about them. In all the community they really were the only ones who ever checked on Priscilla and Noah over the years. For most people, they were just fodder for gossip and strange looks. Even Aunt Prissy's friends only seemed to stop by to catch her up on the latest gossip and dig for more information about her own circumstances but did little to help. For that reason, Noah trusted few people but was finally warming up to the Thomas's.

One day Ruth summoned up the courage to ask Noah if he'd consider joining her at church one Sunday. The thought of him sitting next to her, all eyes on the mysterious handsome boy everyone had heard stories about, made her cheeks pink with delight. Noah on the other hand was quite nervous at the idea. He had never actually considered attending church but since he felt indebted to Ruth and her family, he promised to think it over. But Noah wasn't sure he could subject himself to possible ridicule just as he was gaining courage.

He then thought of Leah. She remained much as Noah always knew her to be—oddly, content in her silence.

She never seemed to mind the way people perceived her and he wondered why he should care so much if she didn't. He also admired the way Ruth cared for her despite the little she got in return from her sister. She shielded her from any potential cruel taunts from her peers and always made sure she was bundled properly, had enough to eat and drink while the adults were distracted in conversation, and helped to find her shoes when it was time to go (which were usually hidden in two separate places). Her patience and protective instinct were touching, and Noah felt certain he could trust Ruth to help him face his fears, should he decide to go to church after all.

As for Everett, Noah had seen very little of him since Lily's going away get-together. One unseasonably warm day while walking in the woods on a familiar-looking trail (according to Lily's description) he stumbled upon Everett and Flora who were up in a tree, hooting and hollering down to him as he passed. The noise startled him at first until he looked up to see their familiar faces. They all had a good laugh and the siblings came down to say hello.

Flora was in a happy mood as usual, while Everett was a little more morose than he had seen him previously. It occurred to Noah that he was trying to appear upbeat but that something was bothering him. He didn't feel comfortable enough to ask him what it was, but he had a feeling he already knew the answer.

Everett asked Noah if he was interested in seeing the view from up in the massive oak tree, but it seemed a little too risky for him still. After much prodding and getting nowhere, Everett instead suggested the three of them take a walk together. Flora seemed to go along with anything Everett said. It was obvious how much she looked up to her older brother and was merely content knowing he wanted her to tag along.

They continued along the trail for a while when the air suddenly began to feel chilly as the shady woods grew dark and dense, blocking out most of the midday sun. Noah shivered. He was gaining strength by the day but was still vulnerable to even minor changes in temperature. Everett took notice and to Noah's relief, led them out of the woods and onto the coastline. The newly freed rays of the sun felt toasty on Noah's skin and his body temperature quickly recovered. As they walked on the beach back toward home, they stopped a moment to take an opportunity to rest on a large piece of driftwood. Flora wandered off a bit to collect shells instead, something she said she watched Lily do often.

Noah walked around the weathered log and gently sat on it while Everett leaped over it with ease before sitting. Once settled, Everett looked silently out at the horizon, deep in a thought…or a memory. Noah recognized that look and finally spoke.

"I miss her too…" his voice trailed.

"Yeah, she was pretty great," Everett replied simply.

And like that, Noah wasn't jealous anymore. He was just glad to have someone to share his pain with. Someone who also understood the hole Lily left behind.

CHAPTER TWENTY-ONE

The following week Noah received his first letter from Lily. He had just finished his lunch when Aunt Prissy brought the mail in. She handed him the letter with a knowing smile across her face, certain of how happy Noah would be to receive it. He tried to appear nonchalant when he took it from her hands, but once he closed the door to his sitting-room he flew to his sofa and tore it open immediately. His eyes lit up with anticipation as he began to read.

My Dear Noah,

How have you been? Things have been going fairly well for our family in Boston, though I miss Newland terribly. I remember when papa first announced we were moving to Maine. I was a little disappointed to leave our home in Virginia, but I never felt the sadness and loneliness that I do now. Isn't it funny how you can live somewhere for only a short time and it has a greater impact on you than living in one place for many years?

We have finally settled in our new home, though it is not quite so cozy as the blue cottage. It is what people call a brownstone, or a townhouse, and it's in a nice neighborhood right in the city. It's quite beautiful, especially when the lanterns on the street are lit up at night, but the houses are all pushed up next to each other and there are not many places to roam, though papa tells me there is a nice park a few blocks from here that we will visit soon.

Speaking of papa, he has started his new job and is managing well, but I think even he was sad to leave Newland. He seemed to enjoy slowing down a bit and didn't seem eager to jump back into his career, but he said the money was too good to pass up. Mama is happy about the money too but dislikes having to start over making all new friends. She says the Boston elite are snobs but everyone I've met so far seems nice. I am sure it won't be long before she'll take up some cause as she is never idle for long, especially now that I am old enough to help around the house and look after myself. Sometimes I wonder why they didn't have more children, but they never talk about it, so I never thought to ask.

Anyway, I am curious to know, how is everyone back in Newland? You're the first person I've written to since getting settled so I am expecting you to fill me in on all the latest. I hope you have made a full recovery by now. I am still amazed by the strides you were making and look forward to hearing more about your ongoing progress. I know your Aunt Prissy was having a hard time when we left so I am especially anxious to hear how she is doing too and how she is managing these big changes. I pray for you both every day.

How do you feel about classes starting

back up? I'm not as excited as I'd like to be, though I think it will be a good distraction. All I can think of is how much I miss Newland and when I can go back. As it is, I spend most of my days at home helping mama get the house in order. I have also found quite a bit of time to paint and read, which helps pass the time. I am seeing a definite improvement in my art when I compare it to where I was even just a few months ago. Of course, I have you to thank for that.

I just finished reading "The Secret Garden" by Frances Hodgson Burnett. Have you ever read it? I really think you'd like it as much as I do. It speaks a lot about friendships in a way that I find relatable and so I wished to share it with you. I hope you'll get a chance to read it and tell me what you think.

Today the weather is quite fair and so mama has decided we should venture out into the city this afternoon, which should make for a bit of an adventure. I've never lived in a city quite as big as Boston, so I'm curious about it all, though I know it won't compare to the beauty and enchantment of the blue cottage by the sea. Big *cities may have their thrills, but I think I prefer the peace and solitude of a small town. If ever given the choice, I believe Newland is where I would live out my days. Do you suppose I will ever have that chance again?*

Well, I'd better run. Mama is getting impatient with me and I want to send off this letter when I go into town. Give everyone my love and know I'll be thinking of you daily. Please write back soon, it would mean so much to me to hear from a friend!

Sincerely Yours,
Lily Stephens

P.S. After reading the book I'm inspired to grow a little garden of my own. We have a small patch in the backyard mama said I could use. Ask Aunt Prissy her secret for keeping her flowers so brilliant!

Noah set the letter down, feeling both happy and sad. It was great to hear from Lily, but difficult to once again face the fact that she was so far away and not returning any time soon. He disliked hearing how lonely she was and wanted to write back straight away, but decided to read the book first, as he already happened to own a copy in his library. He supposed he never read it because it seemed like more of a girl's book, but for Lily's sake, he was willing to give it a try.

A few days later he was pleased to report he did, in fact, enjoy the book as Lily promised and decided to write and tell her so. Perhaps Aunt Prissy might even allow him to accompany her to town to mail the letter. If Lily could face a big city like Boston, then surely, he was ready for the small-town bustle of Newland.

My Dear Lily,

You have no idea what joy your letter has brought to me! I asked Aunt Prissy about her flowers and she told me to let you know that now is the time to plant any seeds you want to come up next spring and not to plant perennials any later than early fall. She said her secret for keeping her flowers bright and healthy is to toss crushed eggshells and coffee grounds into the beds regularly. I thought that sounded a little strange, but she swears by it!

You'll be happy to know, I did read "The

Secret Garden" as you recommended. Fortunately, I already had a copy in my library and was in need of a good read, so I started in right away so that I might report my findings. While I enjoyed the book very much, I do hope you do not liken me to that spoiled brat Colin in your mind! Not that I wouldn't deserve it in some ways, but still, I'd like to believe I fair better in your eyes than that. Of course, the saddest part for me was the scene where he reconciles with his father. Unfortunately, I may never have the chance to set things right with my own. I think of him often and have even gone through some of my old letters from him recently and realize he was a very sad man. I hope to not be consumed with grief as he was. I know with your friendship I never should. There will always be a bright spot in my life.

Speaking of which, you would be proud of me. I have been out exploring a good deal and have happened upon many of the spots you talked about. They are just as you described! Of course, I wish I could share in that experience with you, but it will have to be enough that your spirit is a part of it. You were right about the magnificence of the *tall oaks, how light filters through the birch trees at midday and casts a glow like fairies on the forest, and the amusing little squirrels in the clearing. I spend a good deal of time examining the tidepools as well. All of it was as I imagined it would be! While out on one of my walks I even stumbled upon your good friends Everett and Flora and spent the afternoon with them. I am happy to say they are as good-natured as you claimed, though we spoke far too much of how we all missed you.*

As for my studies, I am intensely looking forward to pouring my heart and soul into my education this year. I realize how much time I've wasted allowing myself to fall behind. It's time to start anew. I believe Aunt Prissy feels the same. You will be pleased to know she is doing much better and is becoming far more lenient than I ever thought possible. Once again, I owe so much of that to you...I truly can never thank you enough for what you've done for us both.

I am very much looking forward to hearing about your shopping trip in Boston and hope you will report back soon. Until then, I am thinking of you.

Your Friend,
Noah Sullivan

CHAPTER TWENTY-TWO

I t was September now and Noah was fully engrossed in his studies. He continued his schooling from home with his usual tutors and they all noticed a significant difference in both his interest and attitude regarding his education. Noah found the world to be a fascinating place and the more he focused, the more he excelled in every subject.

Though Noah was long healed and becoming healthier by the day, as well as Aunt Prissy, Ruth still came around often to help out and just visit. Noah didn't think much about the fact that her assistance was no longer necessary, he was just happy to have the company. She too was well into her own homeschooled classes and as long as she kept up her grades and chores her mother would generously allow her more time to sew and help out at the church in new ways. In fact, she had recently taken up crochet and knitting and was working on scarves, hats, mittens, and blankets for some of the poorer residents for the upcoming winter season.

One afternoon she stopped by and in her hands was a neatly wrapped box with a blue silk ribbon tied around it. Noah gave her a puzzled look when she handed it to him. "C'mon, open it!" She replied with a hint of excitement.

Unaccustomed to receiving gifts, Noah couldn't imagine what it might be. He took a seat then carefully untied the ribbon and pulled the paper away to reveal a simple box. He lifted the top and was pleasantly surprised to find an expertly knitted tan scarf and matching hat. "What's this for?" He asked in surprise.

"Happy Birthday, silly! I hope you like them. I made them especially."

Noah smiled brightly. "Wow, they are incredible!" He exclaimed while trying them on right away. "I don't think I ever had a need for a hat and scarf until now. Never really got a birthday gift from a friend before either. Thank you, Ruth."

Ruth smiled cheerfully in return, pleased with herself for making Noah so happy. Noah arose to give her a friendly hug and as they embraced, they lingered a bit longer than ever before. He liked the warmth of feeling Ruth pressed against him. He had enjoyed affection so little in his young life. He also liked the sweet fragrance of her hair tousled against his cheek.

Noah had almost forgotten himself when suddenly he heard Aunt Prissy calling his name as she knocked on the sitting-room door. Startled, Noah quickly pulled away from Ruth and took off the hat and scarf, tossing them on the sofa. "Come in!" He called out, his voice cracking slightly.

"Noah, Noah," she exclaimed as she entered. "A package came for you!" Without even taking notice of Ruth or the unwrapped contents of her gift, she handed him a brown shipping box. "Bet you can guess who this came from?" She said with a knowing wink.

Noah blushed furiously and set it down on the table next to his sofa.

Aunt Prissy was puzzled by his disinterest at receiving the package. "Well, aren't you going to open it?" She pressed.

"Later," Noah said, giving his aunt a look and then trailing his gaze to Ruth. She wasn't always the most astute individual, but Aunt Prissy seemed to get the hint. But Ruth was all too aware of whom Aunt Prissy was implying the package was from.

Secretly her heart sank a little. It was quite obvious to her and everyone how much Noah cared for Lily—and she for him. She considered her a fine girl—lively and enjoyable company—but over time Noah was becoming important to her as well and she began to have hopes of her own. Still, Ruth had no intention of showing how she felt. With everything Noah had been through the last thing she wanted was to put pressure on him. Not to mention Lily was no longer in Newland and she was.

"It's okay, you can open it if you want." She said, breaking the awkward silence. "I'm going to help Aunt Prissy prepare tonight's dinner. I hope you don't mind if my family joins us. We wanted to do something special for your seventeenth birthday. I've invited Everett and Flora over as well, so they'll be joining us too."

Noah gave Ruth a reassuring grin and with a forced upbeat tone responded, "That sounds great! I'll be in the kitchen in a moment then."

Noah was relieved when Ruth and Aunt Prissy left the room and wasted no time grabbing for the package from Lily, opening it quickly. It had been a couple of weeks since he heard from her and he was excited to see what she might have sent him. He pulled out a carved wooden figure of Peter Pan flying hand in hand with Wendy and an engraving on the base displaying a quote. "The moment you doubt whether you can fly, you cease forever to be able to do it." There was also a note attached that read:

> *Happy Birthday Noah, I found this figure while on a shopping trip in town and it made me think of our favorite book. I wish you continued success in your studies and everything else you do. I believe in you. But no matter how much you grow, never grow up completely. I'll always cherish the boy inside.*

Noah's heart melted with the thoughtfulness of the present and the quote. He rose and set it on a shelf where he could see it often, placing it next to a pretty seashell Lily gave him on one of their first visits as friends. He picked up the seashell and put it in his pocket as a reminder to think of that day later when he had a moment of solitude. He left the scarf and hat thoughtlessly where he had dropped them.

It was agreed that Noah's birthday dinner was a pleasant time had by all. It was the happiest and carefree he had felt in a long time. There was much chit chat and laughing among them throughout the evening. Noah was glad to see how quickly Everett and Flora accepted Ruth as a friend and made the effort to engage her. It didn't entirely surprise him, considering how easygoing and fun-loving they were by nature, but he was even more pleased with how much Ruth seemed to enjoy their company in return. At one-point, Everett raised his eyebrows at Noah over the dinner table, a teasing indicator that he recognized Ruth's beauty. Noah felt a bit uncomfortable at the implication that he assumed the two of them were an item in the making.

Even the Reverend Thomas and his wife seemed to be enjoying themselves and were more friendly and relaxed than he ever knew them. It surprised Noah that they were even willing to take part in a game of charades. It turns out even Reverends like to have a little fun.

It was guys against girls and animals were the topic. Leah and Aunt Prissy decided to sit and watch, though Leah kept meowing like a cat, her favorite animal. Flora proved to be quite good at both impersonating and guessing the animals. She held back nothing when it came to swinging her arm like an elephant's trunk, flapping her arms like a duck, or hopping around like a kangaroo. Everett was of course very good as well, the best of the boys. Naturally, they both had a competitive streak and he and his sister went at it playfully throughout the game to the amusement of the group. Everyone agreed his impression of an ape was the best of the night as he made the perfect face with his tongue pressed against his upper lip, pounded his chest furiously, and jumped on a chair with ease.

Though she lacked natural talent for performance, Ruth managed to be a decent frog, a fish, and a sea lion. Reverend Thomas was in rare form that evening as he impersonated an owl and a billy goat (everyone laughed when he bleated by mistake). Mrs. Thomas managed a respectable giraffe, using her arm as the neck and pretending to eat leaves out of a tree, using her other arm.

Noah was quite nervous at performing the impersonations, due to having all eyes on him, but even he got a good laugh while doing a hippopotamus that everyone thought was an alligator. He was the best at guessing though and won his team the most points. By the end they stopped keeping score altogether amidst all the laughing, teasing, and overall good time they were having.

Noah had never felt so much like a normal teenage boy before, just as he was becoming a man. He was like a whole new person in many ways. There was still something missing though. That evening after everyone went home, Noah helped his aunt to bed and cleaned up the dining room and kitchen. Aunt Prissy remarked more than once that she had never seen so much excitement in the house and by the end of the evening, she was thoroughly exhausted. Noah was thankful for a few moments of reflection before his birthday officially came to an end.

After cleaning up, Noah went out onto the terrace and looked out to the sea. It was too dark to see much, but he could hear the crashing waves echoing across the shoreline. The chill of the night air made Noah shiver and he stuck his hands in his pockets to get warm when he felt the seashell he placed there earlier—Lily's seashell. He pulled it out and examined it carefully then squeezed it tight in his hand and said out loud, "Oh, what a perfect day it was." He was not referring to his birthday.

CHAPTER TWENTY-THREE

The months passed quickly as Noah continued to focus more on his schoolwork and painting. He continued to improve and was moving through his courses at a rapid rate. The areas he once lagged in he now excelled, and his tutors couldn't say enough encouraging things. They were astounded by just how sharp and capable this once lazy, complacent boy, was turning out to be. All impressed upon him that if he kept it up, he might even get a scholarship to a prestigious school. Noah still wasn't sure what he would go to school for though. Other than painting and hoping his father would teach him the fishing trade, he never gave much thought to any other vocation.

Christmas came and went and somehow Ruth managed to talk Noah into being a shepherd for the live nativity. He said he only agreed because he didn't have to speak, but in truth, it was the least he could do after Ruth had been so gracious toward him and his aunt the past few months. Ruth was especially proud of the fact that he got to wear one of the costumes she made, which he complimented several times.

Ruth was Mary and a curly-haired boy named Wade Anderson played Joseph. Wade was normally quite outgoing though it was obvious he thought much of Ruth and became nervous in her presence. Ruth enjoyed his attentions but pretended not to care about it in the least when Noah was around.

Leah was an angel, though she often wandered off from her post without thinking. Ruth would realize she was gone and find her sitting in a corner alone, but Leah always complied without much fuss when Ruth led her back by the hand. After the third and fourth time, Ruth and Noah would exchange a knowing smile which made her heart melt.

Despite his hesitancy, Noah enjoyed himself and he and Aunt Prissy even went to church for the candlelight service on Christmas Eve. He had heard the story of Jesus' birth before but was puzzled when the Reverend also referred to God as Father when he opened the service in prayer. Noah never considered God in such an intimate way and wasn't sure how he felt about calling Him Father, especially since his relationship with his own father was so full of pain and confusion. He asked Ruth about this, but she'd never given it much thought either and just accepted it because her father knew so much about the Bible.

Noah and Lily still wrote to each other regularly, though with school and the holidays it was becoming less frequent, but he decided to ask her about this too since she seemed to mention praying often. He explained to Lily that the more he thought about it, that it made sense since God felt absent to him much of the time and his own father had been distant all his life. Lily assured Noah that God was not absent but always by his side and that He was the one who really helped him with everything in the past year. Noah wasn't sure if he could believe it, but even he couldn't deny the miraculous changes taking place in his life.

Noah applied himself to such a degree that he was able to complete his entire year of schooling by Christmas and was becoming more restless than ever. Still unsure of what his focus should be, but hungry for new experiences, he decided he would take a job in the spring working at one of the markets in town. He didn't need the money—his father had left them enough to survive on for quite some time—but he wanted to know the satisfaction of a day's work and begin earning a living, so he'd be ready when the time came to start a career and support a wife and a family.

Until that time, the harsh winters of Maine kept everyone inside for the most part. The sea strand had accumulated quite a bit of snow and was iced over, so Noah missed the sound of the crashing waves from his terrace door. Instead, he took joy sitting by the fire, reading, and of course, painting. Spring would be here soon enough, and he wanted to make sure the painting of Lily was fully repaired by then since she told him they might be out in the spring for a visit. He hadn't much chance to work on it until then due to his assignments, but now he was carving out a bit of time every day to get it right.

Surveying the painting again brought Lily back to the forefront of Noah's mind. Not that he ever forgot her, but in truth, she was not writing as often and therefore had been occupying less and less of his thoughts. He feared that one day she might only be an apparition, even now her features were less clear in his memory. Getting the red marks totally removed proved to be a challenge as he had to be very careful not to affect the work around it. He no longer had his model before him to help fill in the gaps of his memory. Still, he felt it was coming along quite nicely.

After the Christmas Eve service, Noah and Aunt Prissy began attending Reverend Thomas's church on a weekly basis. They put off considering it for so long and now Noah didn't even know why. After Lily's thoughtful reply to his questions, he figured for him it was the fear of facing God after so many years of ignoring His existence. Now he wasn't scared at all for some reason. He enjoyed singing the hymns and learning what was in the Bible for himself. Sure, he had heard some of the stories like Adam and Eve, Noah, Moses, Samson, and David and Goliath, but it turned out the Bible was yet another thing he was painfully ignorant about. Now he hungered for more knowledge of scripture and even began reading it daily. God no longer felt so distant as He once did, and Noah was reminded everyday of how much he'd missed out on as His world became more and more alive to him. His scope was now so much grander than the boy of sixteen.

Aunt Priscilla was learning a great deal as well, such as how to trust in providence through life's uncertainties, overcoming fear, and how to serve others. The baskets she was once the recipient of she now helped Mrs. Thomas pack and deliver to other members of the community. It was through the delivery of one such basket that she met a gentleman who was a recent widower, and she began to visit him often.

The man's name was Buck Simmons, and he took quite a liking to her, quirks and all. He was a caregiver by nature, he had lovingly nursed his ailing wife for years, but was now feeling lonely and aimless. Priscilla was not a strong woman and quite needy, but she was caring and loyal. They became fast friends and soon they were sitting together in Sunday services. He even came to call on her at Birchwood Cottage a couple of times.

March arrived and Noah had put the final touches on his nearly lost work of art. He wasn't sure if it was his imagination, but it appeared even more beautiful than before. The closer spring approached, Noah's thoughts turned more to Lily and he became anxious to hear news of her family's arrival. This was the moment he'd been pinning his hopes on for months and he felt ready to present to Lily the new person he was becoming.

The ice had not yet melted from the shore, but spring brought about an earthy scent that told it wouldn't be long. The days were getting a bit longer and the markets were buzzing more than they had since the New Year and Noah was ready to start his job. He decided to spend the next few months getting a head start on his final year and saving up money. With any luck, he could take courses through the summer and graduate a year ahead of schedule. Who knew what would come next, but he was driven to make up for the time he missed.

When Everett caught wind of Noah working at the market, he decided to join him on the job front as well. His family wasn't nearly as well off and he knew they could use the extra money, plus one less mouth to feed. Everett had taken his education as far as he wanted to go, and while he was indeed very clever, he was not quite the scholar Noah was shaping up to be. His grades were average, but then he had no use for subjects like history and geography. His interests were more physical in nature, namely building things, so he felt now was the time to seek employment opportunities where he could and hoped to one day land an apprenticeship.

Despite their differences, Noah and Everett got on very well and neither had many male companions so in time became like brothers. Like Flora, Everett would tease Noah often, which was wearing at times, but he learned to accept this about him. At work, however, it became a bit of a distraction as Everett liked to goof around a lot. That was fine for Everett since due to his strength he could quickly make up for lost time and still get more done than all the other boys. For Noah, it was more challenging to keep up, so he finally had to set Everett straight on the matter.

Everett tried to distract him less, but due to his playful nature, he kept up some level of shenanigans, though less frequently. Noah figured at least he made the effort and in truth, he enjoyed his friend's humor and it helped pass the time. It was also nice to have someone to reminisce with about Lily and their hopes for her possible return. This was one topic he never felt comfortable talking to Ruth about. Something told him it would probably hurt her feelings to know he missed Lily so much after the months of friendship they had built since her departure.

Ruth spent a lot of time on her sewing, making simple shifts with pretty fabrics for less fortunate young girls, so Noah didn't see her as often as before anyway. She would still come by occasionally and they would catch each other up on the latest news or he would see her in church every Sunday. Sometimes they even sat together since Aunt Prissy was spending a great deal of time with her new friend, Buck.

There was such comfort between them that Noah knew he count on Ruth any time he needed a friend, but he didn't want to take advantage of her any more than he had to. At least that's what he told himself to alleviate the guilt that was mounting over his renewed occupation with thoughts of Lily. But overall, everything was going along great until a letter was delivered one March afternoon...

To Priscilla Sullivan or whom it may concern,

The fishing boat belonging to your brother, Martin Sullivan, has been located off the coast of Maine, south of Portland. The vessel was found to be abandoned with no crew and showed signs of storm trauma. Our investigation reveals after interviewing several locals who last saw the boat headed out to sea just before a nor'easter struck, that neither Martin Sullivan nor any of the crew survived. We regret to inform you that all are assumed dead. We will be sending along a few of his belongings retrieved from a safe aboard the boat. We are sorry for your loss.

United States Coast Guard

Noah's heart stopped as he read the letter over three times. Then it was final—his father was, in fact, dead and never coming home. Although he fully expected to receive this news, he realized deep down a part of him still held out hope and had not yet accepted the reality of his death. He wasn't sure how Aunt Prissy would take it, as she was doing so much better recently. He really didn't want it to be a step backward.

Thankfully, she wasn't home, so he could grieve in private. How he longed for a warm embrace from Lily. Sure, he had more people in his life than ever but somehow Noah still felt lonely without her. He longed for her peaceful presence and joyful disposition to remind him everything was going to be okay, as she always had. Instead, he went to his room, closed the door, and wept alone.

CHAPTER TWENTY-FOUR

Aunt Prissy took the news about as well as Noah could hope. As expected, she sobbed uncontrollably upon first reading the letter, but recovered her senses much quicker than he expected. It appeared that she too had begun to accept that her brother was gone but the news finalizing the certainty of Martin's death still hurt immensely. Even in his own mind, Noah had allowed himself to hold out a bit of hope and even imagined his father coming home unexpectedly to surprise them, proud of how much his son had progressed since they last saw each other, just like in Lily's book. But Noah knew that was a fantasy more than anything.

All the acceptance in the world didn't stop Noah from feeling a deep need to share his grief with Lily, so he hung on while awaiting news of her arrival this spring. A few days later a letter from Lily finally arrived.

My Dear Noah,

I wish I had better news to share, but my family will not be coming to Maine this spring after all. Apparently, my father was not able to get the time off from work to take a trip at this time. We are still hopeful for an extended vacation this summer, but for the moment I am crushed with disappointment. I was so looking forward to seeing you and everyone else and now I will have to spend my days at home, tending my little garden and thinking of you instead. Please pray things work out this summer...it's just a few more months away. In the meantime, don't forget me. Will write again soon...

Sincerely Yours,
Lily Stephens

Noah knew the situation was beyond Lily's control,

but it was the last bit of bad news he could process. Though he was thriving in many ways, he was also hurting in tremendously. It was too much to bear alone. He choked out the last of a flood of tears he had saved for Lily's shoulder. His sadness had consumed him long enough. He decided to pay Ruth a visit.

Ruth was surprised to see Noah walking up the pathway to her house. While she had spent a great deal of time at his house, he had only been to her house once and that was to pick up some reading materials from her dad. *What could he be up to?* She thought to herself as she watched him through the kitchen window.

Soon he approached the door and knocked heartily. Ruth smoothed out her dress as she entered the small entryway and called back to her mother in the kitchen that she was going to answer the door. When she opened it, she saw Noah panting as though he had been running. He was full of nervous energy and a little wild-eyed.

"Hi Noah, how are you doing? Everything going okay?" Ruth asked.

"As a matter of fact, no. Can we talk for a minute? Privately?" Noah replied, still slightly out of breath.

Ruth looked back into the house and noticed her mother had not emerged from the kitchen to check on their guest. She didn't expect this surprise visit and was unsure of how her parents would feel about it, especially so close to dinnertime. She called to her mother to say she was stepping outside for a few minutes and would be back. Before her mother had a chance to respond she pulled on a wool sweater and was out on the porch, standing with Noah in the cold March air.

"What is it Noah?" She prodded, wrapping her arms tightly around herself to keep warm.

"Please just walk with me a bit, I need to speak to you."

Noah took her by the hand to lead her away from the house and Ruth complied. They walked down the path and past the entrance gate to the quaint Thomas home and onto the tree-lined road.

Once they got a ways from the house's line of sight Noah turned to Ruth, a fire in his eyes. "I'm sorry to take you off guard like this but I needed to see you. Everything has fallen apart and Ruth, you're all I have right now. I got a letter confirming my father is dead and then…then…" He didn't complete his sentence about his disappointment concerning Lily, but his teeth were chattering with sorrow. Then he saw the look of compassion in Ruth's expression and her pretty, red hair cascading down her shoulders. She was a sight for sore eyes. "Well, it just seems like nothing has been right for a long time. I just feel so sad, so terribly sad, and I don't know where else to turn."

Ruth placed her thin white hand on his cheek gently and Noah responded to this affectionate gesture by pulling her close to himself and kissing her firmly on the lips. Ruth was visibly taken off guard by the sudden act of passion, but not unpleasantly so. When he pulled away, she merely blushed.

"I'm sorry if that was unwelcome…" Noah began.

"No, not at all, it's just, I don't know where all this is coming from."

Noah took both her hands in his. "I was having such a hard time today and you were just the first person that came to mind and I had to see you. Then looking at you just now. I hope you'll forgive me."

"Of course, I do," Ruth said quietly. "I'm sorry for everything you are going through, but I'm here for you. Always."

And with that, Noah took her in his arms again, holding her tightly, then looked down at her caring face and kissed her again. He longed to be held as she was holding him now, but somehow, he still didn't feel better. He pushed his doubts aside and walked Ruth back to her house. She was a little anxious about her mother, so she distanced herself from him as they came closer to the door. She put her hand on the knob to enter when it suddenly flew open.

"What's this? Who has come to visit, Ruth?" Her mother asked in a surprised tone.

When she finally realized Noah was standing there she exclaimed, "Oh, hello Noah, what a nice surprise. What brings you here?"

"I just came by to see Ruth for a few minutes. Aunt Prissy and I wanted to invite her over for dinner soon to thank her for all the help she's given us over the past few months. I do hope you'll agree with that?"

Mrs. Thomas was touched by the request. "Dear me, of course! I am sure Ruth would love to come over. She has been so hard at work crocheting baby blankets and booties for young mothers that I'm sure she could use a break. Just tell us when and I'll make sure she's free."

Noah thanked Mrs. Thomas for her kindness, nodded to Ruth, who only stood in stunned disbelief over everything that transpired. Without further delay, Noah waved and set about his way home. Noah's head was swimming with many thoughts, but mostly he was filled with a gnawing sense of guilt. He tried to quiet his conscience for he knew he technically had nothing to feel guilty over, but it was no use.

Lily is three hundred miles away. Who knows if I will ever see her again? She never claimed to love me anyhow. Am I supposed to be alone and unhappy my whole life hoping for something that will never be?

He repeated these words in his mind to soothe himself, but it helped very little. He realized that even though the situation was out of her control, Noah somehow resented Lily for moving away and not being there in his time of need. It wasn't fair or reasonable, but he did. His heart was breaking and now he feared his irrational behavior would once again wreak havoc and cause him to lose Lily for good. He just didn't know what else to do, he felt so powerless over the situation.

CHAPTER TWENTY-FIVE

May was upon them and Noah and Ruth continued to see each other often. She had indeed come over the following week for a special dinner with him and Aunt Prissy, along with Aunt Prissy's new friend, Buck Simmons. They each took a moment to honor her by thanking her for all the help she offered them in their time of need and presented her with a small rose bush Aunt Prissy cut from her garden.

"The trick is to make sure you plant it in the sun." Prissy stressed. "And don't forget to prune them back at the end of the season…"

Noah was just about to cut her off when she quickly changed gears and said she had an announcement. Buck then took over the conversation, proclaiming, "Hold it Priss, this kind of news is a man's prerogative", and politely turned to Noah. "Seeing you're the man of the house now, I thought it only right to get your approval, you see, your aunt and I are engaged to be married and we'd be much obliged if you'd give us your blessing."

Noah couldn't believe his ears, having long accepted his aunt would likely never marry and now moving so fast. His first response was one of concern, but they explained further how Buck was struggling since he lost his wife and Prissy was tired of being alone, so Noah did indeed give his blessing to their delight.

They didn't think it made sense to put it off for long and said a May wedding was what they had in mind. As the news sank in further Noah was relieved in a sense, knowing his aunt would be taken care of by someone with a good reputation like Buck. He was gentle and kind, so he knew she was in good hands. Secretly he wondered if Buck knew what he was getting into, but after having cared for a wife who had many chronic illnesses, he figured the man had been tried and passed the test. Mostly he was thankful his aunt was doing so well and finding a bit of happiness.

A round of hugs was shared by all as congratulations were passed around the table. Ruth had little to add to the news, except that she was happy for them both. She had known Buck all her life and thought well of him, which also put Noah at ease.

The wedding came together quickly and was held at Birchwood Cottage on the terrace due to the intimate nature of the event. The ceremony was short and sweet. A few friends gathered and Reverend Thomas was the officiator, of course. Ruth and Noah stood as witnesses, wearing their Sunday best, and afterward they served a small meal in celebration of the union. Aunt Prissy had never looked happier—her countenance was so different from what it once was. She now glowed with youthfulness and hope for the future. It was an incredible transformation.

After the wedding, Noah was left with an empty house while Aunt Prissy and Buck Simmons headed to an inn down the coast for their honeymoon. Ruth offered to stay with Noah a while longer, but he assured her he would be okay. It was time to face reality—he was on his own. Not quite yet perhaps, his birthday wasn't for a few more months, but after the reading of the will, he was informed that the house and all his father's assets, including the money he saved in the bank, were his when he turned eighteen. There was a condition in the will that Aunt Prissy was to be cared for as long as she was without means to care for herself, but now that she was married to a well-off gentleman that part of the will would be nullified.

Noah still wanted to set aside a little something extra for her, just as a thank you for all she had done for him. Sure, life for the two of them was far from ideal, but he felt sorry for his aunt's state of mind and was just thankful she had loved him through the many years he was alone and was now doing so much better. The doctors she was seeing, combined with their current improved lifestyle, helped a great deal.

After everyone left, Noah looked around Birchwood Cottage with new eyes and felt it took on a new shape. It was no longer the home he knew. Along with the shadows casting from the setting sun, it just felt different somehow. It was quieter than usual.

He walked through the foyer and into the hall and then into his sitting-room and stood before the window he looked out of the first time he saw Lily. The ice had melted along the shore by now and once again the waves crashed along the coast. He walked over to the terrace door and stepped out for some fresh air.

Looking out at the sea he recalled the night he almost drowned. It seemed like a lifetime ago. How much had changed since then—mostly for the better. And yet he missed those summer days sitting on the terrace, laughing and painting and dreaming. Dreams. Noah needed new dreams, but he didn't know what was calling to his heart just yet. For the moment he just wanted to watch the sunset and then rest his mind before work tomorrow.

The following day Noah got up early and headed into town to the market. He had to be there before it opened to pull and pack fresh seafood for display as well as delivery orders. It was hard work, but it was paying off. He was steadily catching up to Everett in terms of workload. His boss even commended him for his progress and work ethic. At first, Noah didn't care for Everett's competitive nature but now was getting into the spirit of the thing and some days even surpassed his workload, much to Everett's chagrin. He also knew work would help him get his mind off things for a while.

It was a chilly walk into town and Noah was glad he brought his warmer jacket. When he arrived, people were buzzing all over the place, setting up their shops for the day.

He loved the excitement of the market. He would often just watch the people as they moved swiftly and gabbed on about their expectations of the day. Everett showed up and asked about the wedding. Noah told him it went very well, to which Everett extended a hearty congratulations.

"So, what are you going to do now?" Everett asked curiously.

"Well, Aunt Priss and Buck are going to stay in the house for a while before I finish school and figure out what I'm doing next. Then they'll probably move into his house when the time comes."

"And what are you going to do about Birchwood?"

Noah paused as he hadn't yet considered it. "I don't really know. I plan to keep it—it's the only connection I have to my father and mother—but it's a pretty big place for one person."

"Well, maybe you won't be alone for long." Everett nudged Noah with a wink.

"Marriage? I don't think so." Noah never even considered it.

"What about Ruth? Seems like you two have a good thing going. She's a sweet girl, not bad looking either. For some unknown reason, she seems to adore you. I'd say you got it pretty good in that department."

Noah chuckled. "Yes, Ruth is a wonderful girl, truly, and yes, she is beautiful, but I think it's way too early to be thinking about marriage. Besides, she has another year of school to complete and I'm just not sure what I want to do with my life now."

Everett shrugged. "Well, I'd hang onto her if I were you. Not much chance a guy like you will get lucky three times."

Noah smirked at Everett's playful remark.

"Anyhow, no use holding out for some ideal that probably doesn't exist. Believe me, I know. As for myself, I'm hoping to snag an apprenticeship working down at the shipyards at the port. I hear there are some openings and I think it would be good to keep my hands busy. Of course, poor Flora will be upset with me leaving but it's time she started hanging out with some girls her own age. Ya know, don't tell anyone, but I think I'm a bad influence on her." He winked at Noah which caused him to laugh.

"You don't say? Truth be told, I think you're a bad influence on everyone you encounter."

Everett gave him his signature boyish grin and pretended to put him in a headlock while he ruffled his hair. "Yeah, don't pretend you wouldn't miss me too!"

"Actually Everett, in all honestly, I would. You've been

a great friend—I mean aside from the fact that I owe you my life—but you've really pushed me in a lot of ways and I'm better for having known you. You'll always be the brother I never had."

Noah wasn't sure he actually saw it, but it looked like he spotted a tear in Everett's dark eyes. "Yeah, yeah you're pretty great too. Now enough mushy stuff. Let's get back to work." That was the first time Noah ever heard his friend be the first to suggest they resume their work.

By the afternoon, the sun was shining and along with the cool breeze wafting from the shore, spring was in the air. Snow still covered the ground in spots, but the sun was rapidly melting them away, leaving the ground wet with puddles. Noah had just finished his work for the day and decided to walk over to the docks to watch the boats coming in. Newland only had a tiny port to bring in supplies, but like the market, it was full of activity.

Something pulled him toward the docks often. Rather than going straight home and hitting the books, he preferred to stop a while and watch the boats drifting in and out. He sat staring at each of them with a sense of fascination, wondering where they had been and where they were off to next. One particular type of boat fascinated him more than all the others though. Its tall sails flapping in the wind, floating gracefully on the horizon and onto unknown places. He had watched these boats with a sense of awe from his terrace since he was a little boy. What adventure it represented in his heart. Noah soon longed for a sailboat of his own.

CHAPTER TWENTY-SIX

The next day after finishing his work at the market Noah went back to the docks to watch the boats again. He observed one particular sailboat pulling in that he'd seen coming and going over the past few months. It was a sleek, white vessel about 38-feet long with the ship name, The Serenade, splashed in blue paint across the backside. A deeply tanned man with a scruffy face of about thirty-five was at the helm, wearing an old captain's hat. Noah watched with curiosity as he steered the vessel into port and prepared it for docking.

He'd seen the man many times, but he was always

alone. He never appeared to be hauling in a catch but seemed to be an ordinary sailor who simply enjoyed being out in the sun. A spontaneous thought struck Noah and when the man finished securing his boat he called out, "Hey, could you teach me how to do that?" It took all Noah had to muster up the courage to say the words.

The man was a bit taken off guard, not certain he was the one being spoken to, but looked around when he finally spotted Noah staring up at him from the dock. "Excuse me, son?" He called out in reply.

"Sailing. Would you be willing to teach me to sail?"

The man scratched his chin as if it were an odd request then hopped off the boat and walked over to Noah. "Well, I never thought about teaching anyone before. Why do you want to learn anyway?"

"It seems like a good skill for a young man to have. Plus, it seems awfully exciting. I'll pay you well."

Noah then made his offer which caused the man's eyes to widen. He was intrigued but still hesitated. "That is a friendly figure, I must admit, but I don't know. You see, I sail alone. What's your name anyway, kid?"

"Noah," he said boldly, becoming more courageous by the moment. "I'm a hard worker and I learn fast. I promise I won't be a bit of trouble, sir."

The man had never been presented with such an offer and was impressed by the determined spirit of the young man. He looked Noah up and down a moment before finally relenting, "I'll tell ya what, if you are really serious about learning to sail then starting this time next Monday, I'll meet with you twice a week and show you the ropes."

Noah couldn't believe his great fortune at being able to start so soon. "That sounds great!" He exclaimed.

"Don't be late kid. If you're not here by three I shove off. Got it?"

Noah nodded in compliance. "I promise, I won't be late. By the way, what's your name?"

"You can call me Conrad," was the name the man gave, then repeated, "Monday at three-o-clock—be here."

"You got it!" Noah called out before the man walked away, disappearing into the crowd.

Noah was so teeming with ideas of new possibilities and flying high that it seemed he was home in no time. Suddenly he felt a renewed sense of purpose—a passion awakening within himself and he couldn't wait to share the news with Ruth. So much so, he planned to head over to see her after he grabbed a bite to eat.

He was so preoccupied with his thoughts that he almost didn't even notice the letter sitting on the floor that had been dropped in the mail slot by the door. He was hanging up his jacket on the wooden coat rack when the back of the white envelope caught his eye. He assumed it was a letter from Aunt Prissy writing from her honeymoon with Buck, so he picked it up casually and turned it around to see it was actually from Lily. His heart fluttered in his chest against his will as he opened it and began to read.

My Dear Noah,

I hope this letter finds you well. It seems so long since I last heard from you. I trust it's because you've been so preoccupied with school, work, and friends that you just haven't found the time. That would be my wish for you anyway. I want so many good things for you, even as my own heart suffers from not being able to communicate more regularly.

I am growing weary of Boston. It's a lovely town, but mama was right, the people have not been quite so welcoming as they were in Newland. However, I have become good friends with a fun girl named Clara who would remind you so much of our dear Flora though perhaps not so very lively. We often take walks together. I've told her a lot about you, and she teases me mercilessly for it. It's nice to have someone to pass the time with, but her family will be moving at the end of the season and then I shall be alone again.

On a positive note, I am continuing to excel in my art, my teacher has told me so regularly and even chose one of my pieces to be featured in the student gallery next month! It's a painting of a sailboat with a boy at the helm. He looks a little like you if you can believe it. I guess most of my paintings are inspired by the sea. I'm still nowhere near as skilled as you, but I'm excited just the same and hope to have the chance to show you someday soon.

But here is the biggest news of all— mama is pregnant! That's right, I'm going to have a baby brother or sister by Christmas, and no one was more stunned than papa. Turns out, mama and papa never thought they could have children, so having me was a real miracle as far as they were concerned. Well, it turns out there is another miracle on the way! Isn't that incredible?

Other than that, I am just trying to

concentrate on my schoolwork as we're heading toward our final exams. Please pray I do well! I still pray for you always. I will write again soon, but I leave you with a quote I heard recently that brings me much comfort…

"True friends, never apart, maybe in distance, but never in heart"

Sincerely Yours,
Lily Stephens

Even in a simple letter, Lily had the ability to stop Noah in his tracks and penetrate his heart. She spoke of nothing particular that should move him so and yet he was rocked to his core with overwhelming emotion. He folded the letter and placed it back in the envelope. He put his jacket back on and proceeded out the door, forgetting his dinner altogether. Noah knew what he had to do.

Before he even reached the pathway that led to the Thomas's home, Noah heard the sound of voices giggling beyond the gate near the shrubs. As he approached, the voices quieted and the curly-haired boy who played Joseph in the nativity emerged holding a small sack along with Ruth, whose cheeks were flushed and smiling. In her hands was a limp bouquet of daisies.

Her face dropped at the sight of Noah, but he was unperturbed. "Ruth, can we speak for a moment?" He asked, determined to fulfill his quest.

Unaware of the reason for Noah's sudden visit, Ruth began stammering. "Oh Noah!" She exclaimed. "Yes, of course! But you remember Wade Anderson, don't you? He just stopped by on his way home and I was showing him to mama's gardens. You see, he hoped to get some rhubarb for a recipe he's trying out tonight. He's an aspiring chef, you know..."

Noah didn't appear the least bit ruffled by Wade's presence. "Yes, sure, I remember Wade." He said, reaching out his hand to shake Wade's, but it was holding the sack. Wade awkwardly switched the sack into his left hand and returned Noah's gesture.

"Nice to see you again, Noah," he said in response then turned to Ruth. "Well, I suppose I should get going. See you Sunday." He called out before trotting down the lane away from the house.

Ruth was still visibly uncomfortable with the incident and began to explain further. "Honestly, Noah, Wade just stopped by completely unannounced and I was just…"

But Noah cut her off. "Ruth, I don't mind about Wade. There is something else we need to discuss."

For the first time, Ruth noticed the dark, serious look on Noah's face and knew he hadn't come to call for a friendly visit. "Okay, would you like to walk then?" She asked, gesturing to the path, when she finally remembered the flowers in her hand. "How about I just put these in the house first?"

"Fine," he replied. "I'll wait here for you."

A few moments later Ruth exited the house and her once rosy cheeks were white. They walked in silence for a short while when Ruth finally spoke. "So, what is it you wanted to speak to me about, Noah?"

Noah dreaded this moment but knew it was better to get it over with. "Ruth, you're a great girl," he began in typical fashion. "I am truly thankful for your friendship over the past few months. And we've grown close in that time, but I'm afraid…" The look on Ruth's face told him she knew what was coming. He still had to finish. "I'm afraid…well, the truth of the matter is…I'm not in love with you."

No matter how much Ruth braced for the words they

still stung with the heat of a hornet. "Why?" She choked out, the tears rising quickly to her eyes.

"It's not you Ruth, honestly. The last thing I want to do is hurt you. Your friendship has been so important to me..."

"Then why?" She asked again, this time more forcibly.

Noah hung his head. "I think you know why. As much as I have tried, I just can't forget..."

"Forget who? You mean, Lily? Must I still live in her shadow even after all this time?" Her words became more bitter with every syllable.

"Ruth, it's not like that. It's just that Lily, she will always hold a special place in my heart and I just don't think it would be fair to continue pretending."

Ruth's eyes were now lit by flames of indignation. "Fair? Do you want to know what isn't fair Noah Sullivan? Being there for you through your darkest times when Lily was nowhere to be found. I gave you everything and this is the thanks I get? Well, you know what, I never want to see your face again. Please leave."

Noah tried to apologize once again but Ruth was hearing none of it. Once again, she asked him to leave and Noah obliged her request, knowing she had every right to feel hurt and angry over the sudden dissolution of their relationship. "I'm truly sorry, Ruth. I hope one day you'll find it in your heart to forgive me," he said before walking away.

"Don't count on it!" She spat back, then turned on her heel to go back to the house. It was over between them, and though it had gone even more terribly than Noah imagined, he suddenly felt light, as though a weight had lifted, and he was free to enter the future come what may. Whether or not he and Lily had a future together remained to be seen, but for now, he could continue loving her without guilt and that was worth everything.

CHAPTER TWENTY-SEVEN

Noah arrived at the docks as planned the following Monday. Though still somewhat troubled over all that had transpired between Ruth and him, Noah was in a jaunty mood and ready to get down to business. Shortly after his arrival, Conrad emerged from the hull carrying a length of heavy rope. "I see you made it!" He called out.

"I'm here and ready to learn!"

Conrad nodded and invited Noah to board his ship. Once on-deck Conrad looked at him with a twinkle in his eyes. "First things first, you need to learn some basic knots." He tossed Noah the rope and so the first afternoon was spent learning to tie a slipknot, a bowline, figure eight, clove, and a scaffold knot.

Afterward, Conrad gave Noah a tour of the boat and explained various terminology and functions of the equipment. It was a lot to take in, but Noah was following along quite rapidly. The more he learned, the more his interest was piqued. Conrad was a good teacher; relatively patient, and good-humored. Even on the first day, he regaled Noah with some tales of his time at sea. He was a self-proclaimed "sea dog" who had been sailing for over ten years and had become quite proficient at it.

Noah also learned that Conrad sailed to many places, but his goal was to one day sail around the world. He often docked in Maine for the summer months, picking up odds jobs and selling goods he'd picked up on his travels, but would move on when the wind turned and head south for the Florida coast. Hearing Conrad's tales created an insatiable hunger in Noah to experience these things for himself one day.

On Thursday of that same week, he was eager to get back to learning. Conrad had given him the piece of rope to take home and work on the knots. He'd spent a good deal of free time working to master them so as to show Conrad the seriousness of his interest in learning. Conrad was indeed impressed with his progress and moved on to show him how to tie a square knot and a barrel roll. They also talked about docking, anchoring, and the points of sail.

At that time Aunt Prissy had also come home from her honeymoon. When Noah told her about his new interest in sailing, she was hesitant to support his decision, but still riding on the waves of marital bliss from the honeymoon, she didn't fight him too hard. Buck was in good spirits as well and patted him on the back for taking the initiative to pursue his passion.

"All boys should learn to man a boat, Priss." He assured her and followed up by sharing a couple of stories from his own time of youth spent aboard a fishing vessel and was proud to say he'd quite enjoyed it—aside from his predisposition to seasickness.

Noah was now several weeks into his lessons and picking it up like a shot. Conrad had even taken him out a couple of times and let him steer and raise and lower the sails. Though a bit intimidating at first, Noah came to really like Conrad the more he got to know him. He was a loner but an easygoing sort of guy, always full of great stories, and a great mentor. Even Conrad himself was surprised how much joy he took in teaching another person. He too took quite a liking to Noah and respected his work ethic.

Noah was getting strong and tan with all the physical

labor of work and time outdoors. He was finally becoming the man he once dreamed of becoming for Lily, but there was still so much unknown about the world and his future that he had yet to explore. His studies would come to an end in a couple of months and then what? There was something exciting about knowing anything was possible.

Almost as if he read his mind, Conrad approached Noah one afternoon while he was securing a sail as they turned westward. "I've been thinking Noah, you've shared a bit about your situation with me and it seems like you're kind of lost about what to do with your life right now. Well, I've enjoyed working with you and I see real promise, so I thought I'd make a proposal. Just something to consider anyway. What would you think of joining me at the end of the season down the coast to Florida? I head that way every winter, like I told ya, and while I'm used to going it by myself, I think it would be nice to have another hand on deck to work things out. You'd learn and see a lot."

Noah was taken aback by the offer and didn't know how to answer right away. "It sure sounds like a great opportunity but let me think about it a bit. I'll let you know soon."

With plenty of time to make a decision, Conrad assured him he was in no rush to get an answer, but Noah didn't need to think very long to reach a conclusion. It all started to make perfect sense to him finally. While his aunt had hopes of him continuing his education, Noah knew that this was the opportunity he had been waiting for—to be able to learn a valuable skill and a chance to see and do so many of the things he'd missed out on. What was left in Newland for him now? He returned the following week with an answer for Conrad that he would accept his offer with a resounding "yes."

As expected, Aunt Prissy was not too keen on the idea, but Buck once again saved the day by expressing the good experience it would be for "the young lad" and how his education would still be waiting for him in a year when he returned.

"But what if he should never return?" Aunt Prissy bellowed, revealing her deepest fear.

Buck persisted. "I should say, look how the boy has become as strong as a mule and always was smart as a whip. If anyone can see it through, young Noah would have as good a chance as any. And I should dare say, Priss, he wouldn't want to stay away from Newland for long. He has a sweetheart waiting after all."

Noah hadn't yet told them about how things ended between Ruth and him just yet. He figured the town gossip would make its way back to Aunt Prissy soon enough, especially with her being so involved with Mrs. Thomas. Now was not the time to share the news, as he didn't need to give her more things to worry about.

Besides, in his heart, Noah did still long to have a sweetheart to return for, but there was still no word from Lily on her family's return to Newland. Then again, sailing had one added benefit—he would sail right to Lily's door in Boston if need be!

CHAPTER TWENTY-EIGHT

I t was the end of June when Noah finally received a letter from Lily informing him that her family was, in fact, coming back to the blue cottage for a couple months. They would be there the first week of July and stay through August. Noah was exceedingly glad of the news, he had waited many long months for this very letter, but now he found himself wracked with nerves. What would Lily think of who he was becoming? What if they had both changed too much in the past year? Could their friendship ever be the same?

His heart was full of trepidation, and despite

overcoming so many fears, it was time to face his greatest fear of all. He didn't know the exact date of their arrival, but knew it was coming soon and then all questions would be answered. With his aunt's help, he prepared the house so that it would be welcoming to guests. He took several walks over to the blue cottage, something he had avoided doing for some time, fearful of the melancholy it brought him. But now he knew it wouldn't be long before the house would come to life again with Lily's captivating spirit to fill its walls.

The days passed slowly as Noah awaited the Stephens's arrival. It was an early evening on the third of July when Noah was passing the hours on the terrace painting. The sun was still somewhat high in the sky but reflecting various shades of pink beneath the clouds on the horizon. He had just finished adorning a leaf with drops of dew on a tree he was working on when he looked up and recognized a familiar vision heading his way along the shoreline.

For a moment it was like he stepped back in time to a year ago and he felt the same allure rise up in him as he watched this enchanting creature run along the sand at the sight of him. For a moment, the young, inexperienced, naïve boy had returned. Had she ever really left at all?

Lily caught sight of Noah and he raised his hand in a wave. She waved back, urging him on. He ran through the yard, past the garden, over the hedges, and onto the seagrass. She too ran toward him and he didn't have to go far before they met on the sand just near the waves.

Without much thought, he threw his arms around Lily and lifted her off the ground in a tight embrace, as if he would never let her go. He held onto her like that for some time before finally setting her down and pulling away to get a look at her face—*that radiant face*. She was really there in the flesh and in his arms. Her brilliant light shining from within and revealing her beauty from without.

Lily was smiling with tears in her eyes at the sight of her dear friend, whom she barely recognized. He had grown up considerably and was strong and so much of life was in his eyes. She was crying now.

"What's wrong?" He asked, a protective concern overcoming him.

"I just didn't know until I saw you if you would be happy to see me again."

Noah couldn't believe his ears. "How could you think such a thing? I've thought of little else since you've left."

Lily blushed and looked away from Noah's gaze. "Well, Flora wrote some time ago and told me about you and Ruth. That's why I hadn't written as much. I thought perhaps you were in love with her and I didn't want to interfere with your happiness. That is until I saw the way you looked at me just now—just as you always had. It was more than I could have hoped for."

Noah hugged Lily tighter to himself. "No, there is nothing between Ruth and me. I mean, there was for a moment, or I should say, I tried, but I couldn't forget you. I could never forget you, Lily Stephens. The only girl I could ever love is here in my arms."

And with that, Noah brushed a stray hair from Lily's face and kissed her passionately on her soft, waiting lips. It was a real kiss, authentic and true, like neither of them had ever experienced until now. It was born from a deep friendship and fueled by mutual passion for one another. Any doubts either of them had up until then had dissipated now that they were reunited in a tender embrace.

Later that evening they sat together in the cool sand, the sun behind the horizon, holding hands as they spoke. Noah explained how he had tried to let Ruth down gently. Ruth was naturally hurt and angry as he explained the truth regarding his undying love for Lily, but it couldn't be helped. He expressed his wish to part as friends, but it seemed she was still angry with him and unwilling to make amends. Rumor had it that she was now entertaining the affections of Wade Anderson, the boy from church who doted on her endlessly.

Lily felt a little better knowing that Ruth was moving on and hoped the incident wouldn't also put an end to their friendship as well, though she was doubtful.

All that mattered now was that they were finally together and had the next two months to enjoy each other without misunderstandings or conflict. Noah shared his plans to sail south with Conrad over the winter months and was glad it would not interrupt their summer plans. Lily was amazed to hear of all the developments since she'd been away but was happy for the opportunity Noah had.

"It's incredible," she mused, "just how far you've come. You really kept your word. You did it. I always knew you could, but you did it all by yourself, Noah."

"No, that's not entirely true. It was always my thoughts of you that urged me forward. Every time I got scared, every time I doubted or was weary from fighting. I thought of you and how I needed to be worthy of you someday."

"I told you, Noah Sullivan, ▨▨▨▨▨▨▨▨▨▨▨▨▨▨ Still, I admire you deeply for everything you've accomplished. Only, I'm sad that we should be separated again soon enough, and then what?"

Noah gazed intensely into Lily's eyes. "I'm coming back for you Lily. When I return, I'm going to do everything in my power to be by your side, even if I have to move to Boston. And then I'm going to do whatever it takes to convince you to marry me and bring you back to Newland and carry you over the threshold of Birchwood Cottage. To have and to hold."

Lily's cheeks turned crimson as she looked down for a moment and then back into Noah's admiring eyes. "It won't take much effort to convince me. I'll be counting the minutes."

Noah kissed her gently on the lips again. They walked back up to the blue cottage where he dropped her off at home. It was hard to release her again, after being parted for so long, but he reminded himself they had the rest of the summer together. Besides, he had a painting to wrap.

Boy, will she be surprised! He thought to himself, smiling as he imagined her reaction when he finally presented her with the finished painting. Noah then walked on toward Birchwood Cottage, but not before turning on the path that headed to the beach. Once out of the trees he looked up at the stars just emerging from the darkening night sky and then to the shore. The ocean called to him at that moment, so he took off his shoes then ran toward the crashing waves and entered.